IT WAS TOO LATE TO RUN NOW . . .

Cody was back at the tree, playing the flashlight around in the snow. In a moment he picked up Rory's trail. He traced it with the light to the edge of the bush and swept the beam once, quickly, among the trees. Then he reached behind his back, loosened something from his belt and hefted it in his hand. Rory's scalp began to prickle. It was a hatchet!

The Mystery at the Wildcat Well

Robert Collins

Illustrated by Douglas Johnson

Previously published as *Rory's Wildcat*

A SECRET CIRCLE MYSTERY

SEAL BOOKS
McClelland and Stewart-Bantam Limited
Toronto

For Cathy and Leslie

This is a work of fiction. The characters, names, incidents, places, and dialogue are products of the author's imagination and are not to be construed as real.

THE MYSTERY AT THE WILDCAT WELL
A Seal Book / published by arrangement with McClelland and Stewart, Ltd.

PRINTING HISTORY
McClelland and Stewart edition published 1965
Seal edition / June 1981

Seal Books acknowledges the contribution of Arthur Hammond, the original Editor of the Secret Circle Series.

ISBN 0–7704–1684–5

PRINTED IN U.S.A.

0 9 8 7 6 5 4 3 2 1

Contents

1

The Voices

In a way, the mystery all began with the ice cream sundae. If Rory hadn't been sitting eating ice cream that day, he'd never have overheard the voices, and if he hadn't overheard the voices. . . .

Anyway, it all began when the fat waiter stopped beside Rory's booth and said, over the noise of the restaurant, "Here it is, kid."

It was a good sundae, the kind the menu called King Arthur's Castle. For a second Rory wondered, Who ever heard of King Arthur away up here in the bush? It came in a glass bowl with two scoops of vanilla ice cream and two thin strips of banana looped around the scoops, then another dip of ice cream, chocolate this time, with little wedges of banana all round cut like spires and towers. And on top of that, a maraschino cherry. Rory reached for his spoon and looked at the Castle. He felt good for the first time since he'd left Edmonton.

"Twenty-seven below zero out there and you eat ice cream!" The waiter was looking out the restaurant window at Fort Mackenzie's main street. It was January and you could almost *see* the cold: crusty snow glittering in the afternoon sun like cake icing, people huddled in parkas with their red noses and frosted eyelashes sticking out, trucks puffing great balloons of frozen exhaust. The waiter shivered and looked back. "I'll be darned if I'll ever understand kids."

The waiter was trying to be friendly, probably. He had one of those round plump faces that wrinkled up in rolls and creases when he smiled. He looked like the drawings of Old Mister Sun in a story book Rory'd had when he was a little kid. But what could you answer when someone said something like that? Some kids would have said, "Whaddya got ice cream on the menu for if you don't want us to eat it?" But Rory's mother had taught him

1

manners, so he decided not to say anything. He'd never known any grownup that really understood kids. Except his mother. Then he began to feel bad again, so he quickly buried his spoon in the sundae.

"You want me to give you the bill?" the waiter asked. "Or will there be something else?"

"My dad'll be along pretty soon. I guess he'll want something."

"Sure," said the waiter. "Uh ... let's see now, do I know your dad?"

He figures I'll try to sneak out without paying, Rory thought. Out loud he said, "He's Mr Millard. Of West-Can Oil."

"Tank Millard, the toolpush? Heavy-set guy with grey hair? He's your dad?"

Rory nodded, his mouth full of banana. He knew a little bit about the oil business: that his dad was a toolpush, for instance, which meant that he was the rig boss. And that everybody up here called him Tank, although he didn't know why. But his dad liked it better than Horace, which wasn't a very hairy-chested name, Rory had to admit.

"Sure," said the waiter. "Tank's been coming up here with his crews and his rigs for three, four winters. Looking for oil like all the rest of them and none of them found it yet." He looked around the restaurant, full of cigarette smoke and clattering dishes and the rumble of men's voices. The rows of booths along each wall and the stools at the counter were filled with men in parkas and high boots. It seemed to be a kind of uniform up here. But, of course, this was the North. Northern Alberta, anyway, with the Northwest Territories just a few miles away. No wonder the waiter thinks I'm weird, eating ice cream.

"This is sure a good sundae. Did you name it?"

"Huh? Oh, no, my little girl did." The waiter smiled to himself. "She's grown up now. Lives in Calgary. But she named it. She even helped me make the first one." The waiter sat down in the opposite seat. "Seems like a long time ago. This used to be a pretty quiet town then.

2

Still is, in the summer. They can't move their oil rigs and trucks over the muskeg unless it's frozen, y'know."

"I don't know, exactly."

"Well, muskeg's soft ground, real soft, sort of like a swamp. The north's full of it. That's why they hunt for oil in the winter. I forgot, you've probably never been here before, eh? Don't I remember Tank saying that you live in Edmonton with your mother?"

Rory stopped eating and looked at the table top.

"I used to. My mother died, five and a half weeks ago."

"Aw, now!" All the creases and wrinkles in the waiter's kind face turned down and now he looked like Old Man Moon. "Aw, I'm really sorry to hear that. Well, so you're going to live here. On the rig, with your dad?"

Rory nodded.

"Well . . . " The waiter forced a grin. ". . . you won't have to go to school anyway."

Rory tried to grin back. "I *will*, sort of. My teacher back in Edmonton was real nice. She made up a bunch of lessons for me over Christmas—she said I was a special case—and said if I studied hard and could come back and write exams next spring, maybe I'd get my year."

"Well, anyway, you'll be in the north with a real oil rig and not many kids can say that. It get's pretty lively around here when they're hunting oil, y'know. All the companies are trying to find out what the others are doing. Secrets, secrets! Boy, this town is full of secrets! Bet you're excited!"

"Not so much as . . . as kind of scared."

"Yeah? Oh, don't worry. Most of these guys look rough but they're not so bad. Tank'll take good care of you. He sure makes his crews behave. Wish I could say the same for some of the others." The waiter stood up and stretched. It was then that the voice spoke up from the booth behind Rory. "Hey, Fatso, we ordered two pieces of pie. Do you wait table or do you just stand around yakking all day?"

It was a harsh, unpleasant voice and, for an instant, it made Rory pause in mid-swallow: he wondered what it was about the voice that bothered him. The waiter said,

"Awright, awright" and fetched the pie. There was a jingle of coins from the booth and the voice said sarcastically, "Keep the change. The service here is great!" The waiter stomped back to his counter without a word.

Rory gave a little sigh of relief. He forgot about the voice and dug into the sundae again, circling round the cherry, leaving it for the last. The waiter was nice enough, but he hadn't understood. He didn't know that when Rory said "scared" it didn't mean scared of the men or of falling off a truck or of wolves or anything like that. It meant . . . well, Rory didn't know exactly, except that he had a strange uneasy feeling: not just any feeling, but a special one he'd had before. And every other time he'd had it, something bad had happened.

Like the time long ago, when he'd felt this way and told his mother, and the very next day someone had poisoned Clancy, their Boston terrier. Then, a couple of years after that, he'd dreamed about a fire so real that he'd waked his mother. There had been no sound, no smoke in the house, but when she'd gone downstairs to show him that everything was all right, a fire *was* just beginning to smoulder on the carpet, in front of the fireplace.

After that his mother had said, half seriously, that maybe Rory had—what was the word?—premonitions. It meant that maybe he could see into the future. Rory's father, when he came home from one of his drilling jobs, was pretty angry when he heard about it. "Don't fill the boy's head with nonsense, Moira," he had said.

But his mother had said that it wasn't nonsense, that Grandfather Rory Mulveen had had the gift of predicting the future and that people had come for miles around in County Kildare to get his advice. Rory's mother was from County Kildare. She'd come to Canada with her parents on holiday to see the Rocky Mountains. Their rented car had broken down on a back road and the first man to happen by and help was Tank Millard. Well, one thing led to another, Rory's mother used to say afterward when she re-told the story, and the big quiet man who'd been chasing oil wells all over the world fell in love with the laughing Irish girl barely half his age.

4

But she'd never stopped loving Ireland. She told wonderful stories about fairies and leprechauns. And she had black hair and freckles, and she could laugh or sing or cry with children and never be embarrassed about it the way most grownups were.

Finally there had been that day five and a half weeks ago. He had just come home from school and his mother was going out. Suddenly—Rory didn't know why—he had run to the door and begged her to stay. She'd smiled and tweaked his ear and said, "Here you are, nearly as big as me, and starting to take care of me. I'm glad! Well, I'm just off to the store. Be back in a shake."

But she'd been gone a long time and Rory hadn't really been surprised when the policeman came, finally, with a neighbour and awkwardly told how a car had gone through a pedestrian crosswalk just as his mother was crossing. . . .

Rory blinked hard and blew his nose. Maybe he just felt bad because everything was upside down; his mother was dead, the house was sold, Christmas had been a real mess, and, after that, when his father had come back here, Rory had stayed with neighbours. And now he was here, waiting for a father he hardly knew.

The few times they had been together, it had always been hard for Rory to find things to say to his father. He knew his father didn't enjoy the meetings either. After all, he was *old*, nearly fifty! He'd forgotten how to talk to kids, or maybe he never knew.

Look at right now, for instance. Rory had got up at six o'clock to catch a plane from Edmonton to Peace River. But his father hadn't been waiting at the Peace River airport. Instead, a man with "WestCan" on his cap said, "Your dad asked me to give you a lift, son. He's pretty busy but he'll meet you in the restaurant at Fort Mackenzie, soon as he can."

But Rory knew that his father was really just putting off the meeting because it would be awkward, as usual. So they'd gone by truck up the lonely Mackenzie Highway for nearly six hours. Some beginning!

He ate the maraschino cherry and leaned back. A half-dozen of the noisiest crewmen had left the restaurant

5

and there was a small lull. Then he became aware of the voice in the booth behind him. It was lower now, but still strange and hard. It reminded him of flat stones hitting together, and it came clearly through a crack between the booth and the wall.

"Listen," the voice said. "I don't want 'ifs' and I don't want 'maybes.' I want that information. Understand?"

A second man answered, but so low that Rory could only hear a deep murmur.

"Sure, it's risky," the first one replied. "But you'll be right handy to everything. You can find out everything we want, and you'd *better*!"

The second man muttered again.

"Oh, you 'didn't know scouts worked the way I do,'" mimicked the first. "Well, let me tell you something. There's scouts and there's scouts. A lot of people don't like my methods, but I get results. When somebody hires me to get information, I get it. I don't care how, but I get it."

Silence. Rory shivered and huddled lower. He was glad these old-fashioned booths had high backs, not like the low ones in city restaurants. Certainly the two men didn't know they were overheard, which was just as well. It was a cruel, vicious voice, that first one. There it was again. . . .

"You stand to make ten thousand bucks from this. But don't try to back out. Because you won't just lose ten thousand bucks, mister, you'll lose your health."

Another silence. The restaurant still hummed with business, but it was all in the background now. Rory's ears were tuned to the little drama behind him. He heard the scratch of a match and smelled fresh cigarette smoke through the crack.

"Now remember, I want everything. I want to know when they spud in and how deep they are every couple of days or so. When they start coring, I want to know the results. And if they get a show of oil, mister, I want that news real fast, because my people will want to get land. You understand? I want all that, and if you have to stay up nights or steal or rough somebody up to get it, well, you do just that."

Rory's brain was whirling with the words: "spud in,"

6

"coring," "get land"—strange words that he didn't understand. But there was no mistaking the threats. And there was no doubt that he was sitting right on top of a mystery and that the man with the harsh voice was some kind of spy. He was still talking.

"No, I don't know how you'll get in touch with me. I don't know where I'll be, stupid! We don't even know where *you'll* be, until they set up the rig, now do we? But I'll be around, and when you get settled I'll let you know where I am, somehow. Hold on, that's him coming through the door! Quick, out the back way! He knows me. Mustn't see us together."

There was a scurrying in the booth. Rory dared not turn his head. He stared straight out into the darkening street. A cluster of men poured through the door, and—he heaved a sigh of relief—one of them was his father. Tank Millard, broad and solid in his parka, a cap with ear-flaps pulled low on his face, stamped into the restaurant. He looked around, saw Rory, nodded and waved. Then he stopped for a word with the waiter.

Only then did Rory slowly, gingerly, turn in his seat and put an eye to the crack. The seats behind him were empty. The pair had fled. But who were they? And who was the "he" coming in the door that had scared them off?

He went over it again in his mind, quickly. They were spies, for sure. It had something to do with oil—the man had mentioned "a show of oil," whatever that was.

Suddenly Rory had an enormous thought. Was the "he" his own father? Was it Tank Millard's rig the men were talking about? Were they going to spy on his rig? "You'll be right there handy to everything," the man had said. Was it possible there was going to be a spy right on his father's crew?

2

Rough-House

Rory's father came toward the booth, calling back to the waiter, "Just a black coffee for me, Chub." He was not tall, maybe five foot ten, but his shoulders and arms were huge and his hands were half as big again as the average man's. His face was square, like the rest of his body, and he had little wrinkles round his eyes from years of squinting into the sun.

When he took off his cap, his hair stuck up in the back. Rory automatically ran a hand over his own head; he had the same kind of hair. That was about the only thing that was the same about them, he thought.

For an instant Rory thought of telling him about the strange conversation. Then a warning voice inside him said, Not yet. What can you prove? You think it's your father's rig and it might be one of his crew but you don't know.

Anyway, his father hated wild stories. Rory remembered the time when he had been just a little kid and had made up a game in which he was a kind of super-detective who worked for the RCMP, the FBI and Scotland Yard whenever their regular men were stuck for ideas. But his father, when he found out about it, said, "Why don't you get out in the fresh air and play a *real* game?"

It was that way with everything. If Rory said he'd read there was life on Mars, or that you'd be able to press a button on the telephone when you were at work and turn on the oven at home, or that someday there'd be a colony on the moon, his father got sarcastic.

"Between you and the books, Moira," he'd say to Rory's mother, "the kid's turning into a real odd-ball. All imagination and no facts. Can't trust a thing he says."

Now, Tank Millard stripped off his parka, looked down at Rory and managed a forced-looking smile.

"Well, how's it going?"

9

Feeling all the old awkwardness rise up between them again, Rory said simply, "Things are okay."

His father slid into the opposite seat.

"The neighbours treat you okay?"

"Yes. They tried to be nice."

"Uh . . . have a good trip?"

"Pretty good. I had to get up real early."

"Well, I'm afraid you'll be up early every morning from now on. Things are a little tougher out here than in those story books of yours."

Would he ever stop saying "those books of yours" as though it were a crime to read? Rory wondered. Out loud, he said, "I'll make out all right."

His father sipped the hot coffee.

"I hope so." He drummed on the table top and looked away, as he always did when he was about to say something unpleasant. "I guess we ought to get something straight, Rory. I can't spend much time with you. It's going to be awkward for both of us. I mean, it's all new to you and it's not very convenient for me."

He looked at Rory now, still not unkindly but rather as though he were talking to a stranger. "I've always believed that family matters should be kept out of a camp. Well, it can't be helped this time. I don't like you living alone or imposing on the neighbours. So this is the best we can do, until we figure out something else."

"I know."

"As long as you behave like one of the crew it'll be all right, I guess."

"I won't get in your way," Rory said stiffly.

"You'll work your shift as kitchen helper the way we agreed," his father went on, as though he hadn't heard. "You'll get wages—not like a man's, because we don't expect you to work as hard as a man, but pretty good wages all the same. You're big enough to be thinking about earning your way."

"That's okay with me."

"I want you to get your schooling, like your mother wanted, but you'll have to manage that on your own time."

"That's okay," Rory said again.

"Fine," said his father, and looked a little relieved, as if he had been afraid that Rory might burst into tears. "Anything else you want to know?"

"Yes. What's 'spudding in' mean?"

Tank Millard looked surprised.

"You never asked me about drilling before. How come now?"

"I heard some . . . some men talking."

"All right." His father took a paper serviette and a pencil. "Now, the geologists have been over this piece of land we're going to see tomorrow. You know what geologists are?"

"Sure. They study the earth."

"That's about right. Well, they've made all kinds of tests and they've told us, 'We think there's oil down there, but you'll have to drill to find out.' So we come along with the drill rig. You know what a wildcat is?"

"It's an animal."

"Yes, but there's another kind. This well we're going to drill is called a wildcat. That means—well, it means it's a kind of wild chance. We don't know what we'll find."

"So why do you want to go there if it's such a big chance?"

His father looked even more surprised, and a tiny bit pleased.

"Well . . . that's what this business is all about. You see, we *have* to find more oil. We keep using it up for gasoline and furnace fuel and jet fuel. And it's running low. There's lots of it over in the Arab countries, but they're always having wars or raising the price, so we can't depend on them. We *have* to find more of our own."

He gulped coffee, and a note of excitement crept into his voice.

"Now what's really fun about this particular job—other companies have drilled where we're going and haven't found a drop. But we think we're smarter. We think they didn't go deep enough. You see, there *is* oil to the south—fields like Zama, Rainbow—and we might just find more. If we do, it'll set the whole industry on its ear."

He drew a tall tower on his serviette.

"Okay, back to your question. We go there and set up

11

this derrick—I guess you've seen pictures of derricks in those books of yours?—and we start to drill. We put a cutting tool, called a bit, on the end of a length of pipe and we start boring into the ground. That's 'spudding in.' "

"What's coring?"

Millard raised an eyebrow.

"You really got an earful from somebody, didn't you? Well, under the earth there's all kinds of rock. Some kinds have oil, some don't. They're at different levels, sort of like layers of cake only not as nice and even. So when we're drilling we stop every now and then to cut samples of rock. We use a bit that looks like a doughnut, and the rock pieces it cuts are round and long, like skinny fence posts. They're called cores, and they're very important. I'll get Oscar Reason, the geologist, to tell you all about it some day if you're really interested. Anything else? I have to get over to the office."

"Just a couple of more things," begged Rory. "What are 'scouts' and what's it mean to 'get land'?"

Tank Millard looked at him sharply. "Where did you hear about that stuff?"

Again, Rory almost started to tell about the voices. But he said, "Oh . . . somebody . . . there were men talking . . . I didn't see who."

"This place is probably full of scouts. Well, this is pretty complicated, but you might as well hear about it. It's a good idea for you to get some solid facts in your head for a change. Chub, how about a hot coffee?" He glanced at Rory's empty dish. "And something for the boy . . . a hot chocolate, okay? Well, you know what scouts were back in Indian days, don't you?" Rory nodded. "They went out to get information. It's something like that here. Everybody's trying to find oil up here. That's our business, finding oil. So most companies have scouts: men who try to find out what the opposition is doing."

"So's they can get land?"

"That's about right. You see, a company can't just drill wherever it wants. Oil's a mineral, just like gold and silver, and up in the Territories the government owns the mineral rights."

He blew on his coffee. "Wow, I asked for a hot one and

12

I got it! Well, first a company gets permission to go in and explore for oil, as we're going to do. Now, come spring, the government's going to put a bunch of that land up for sale. It'll invite a lot of companies to bid. Whoever buys it gets the chance to produce oil from it, if there *is* oil."

He sipped noisily from the cup.

"Okay, suppose we find oil up where we're going. Our company will want to get as much more of the land around there as it can. But the opposition'll do its darnedest to find out if we *did* strike oil, and we'll do everything we can to keep it a secret until we get the land. If they *do* find out, they'll try to outbid us. And there's big money at stake."

"How much?"

"Up here? Oh maybe twenty thousand an acre. For a big tract of land that would run into millions."

"Millions of *dollars*?"

"Sure. This is big business, one of the biggest there is. It costs millions to drill, too, and even then you don't always find oil. It's about the biggest gamble on earth. And that's why there are scouts. Anything they can find out for their company will cut down on the gamble a little bit."

"Boy! This'll be pretty exciting after all!"

"Now wait a minute! Don't go looking for guys skulking around in black cloaks, like in those books of yours. You'll probably never see a scout. Oh, there might be some sitting back behind the trees a quarter mile away, with field-glasses or telescopes. But it won't do them much good because in winter we put big canvas covers around the bottom part of the rig, to help keep the men warm. And that sure spoils it for the scouts. So don't get any wild ideas. And don't go around talking about little men from Mars, either. It'll make us both look pretty silly."

He's spoiled it, Rory thought. I was really interested and so was he, and then he had to say that and spoil it. But Tank Millard, looking at his watch, didn't notice Rory's downcast face. "Migod, look at the time! I have to get over to the office before supper. You go on over to the hotel and I'll see you later."

"Couldn't I come along? Please?"

"Well . . . all right."

13

They rose from the booth. Rory pulled on his brand-new green parka. Suddenly there was a crash of dishes behind them and a cry of "Fight!"

At the far end of the room a man was on his back, another standing over him, and a crowd gathering round. The fat waiter headed for the door, shouting, "One of them's got a knife! I'm going for the Mountie!"

"No, wait, Chub," Rory's father said sharply. "The big guy's from my rig. I'll handle it."

He pushed through the crowd to the back of the room. The man on the floor was sitting up, a tough, lean figure in buckskins, with a ragged grey beard and a tiny trickle of blood at the corner of his mouth. He was clutching a hunting knife with a blade honed wickedly thin.

"You big ugly Polack," he snarled. "I'm gonna slit you right up the belly like a hog."

"Try it!" The man who was standing really *was* ugly, and big, maybe six foot four, with black slits of eyes under bushy brows, a shaggy black moustache and an old white scar that ran from his chin to his left ear. He stood calmly, legs set, waiting.

"Wirkowski!" Tank Millard said sharply. "Leave him be."

The big man frowned but never shifted his eyes from the knife.

"He started it, Boss," he growled. "Now I'm gonna fix his wagon."

"No!" Tank Millard snapped. "And you put away the knife, old man."

Wirkowski hesitated. The other man, up on one knee now, glared over his shoulder at Rory's father. "Keep out of the way or I cut you too, Millard! I told you last year, keep out of my country!"

"It's not your country and nobody's bothering you. Put down the knife."

"You and your stinking trucks and stinking bulldozers!" The man came to his feet, watching Wirkowski. "Tearing roads through the country. Scaring off the game. A man can't make a living on a trapline no more. There ain't no animals for miles."

"I can smell one right here," taunted Wirkowski.

14

"Shut up, Wirkow . . ." Rory's father began, but it was too late. The man in buckskins sprang at Wirkowski. His knife arm came up, underhand, fast. Wirkowski ducked, flailed a roundhouse right at the man and missed. Then Tank Millard had the old man's wrist. He pulled the arm back and squeezed. The man grunted and clawed with his left hand to break the hold. The rig boss tightened his grip. The man gave a little gasp and dropped the knife. Tank Millard kicked it aside. The man looked blankly at his hand and flexed it slowly.

"You nearly broke it," he said.

"You should've let me clobber him, Tank," grumbled Wirkowski. "I'd've broke his neck."

"You just lay off him," said Rory's father. "And you beat it, old man, and be glad I didn't call the Mountie. We don't want trouble with you. You let us alone, we'll let you alone."

The man pushed through the crowd, found his knife, stuck it in his belt, and made for the door. He paused, a hand on the knob.

"You're all the same, ya bloody bandits! Took this country away from the people who live here. Well, I been here thirty years, Millard; you can't take it away from me." His voice was thick with rage. "You ain't gonna get away with it. I'll get even. One way or another, I'll get even."

The door slammed behind him and a little hush fell over the restaurant.

3

Rory's Wildcat

"Gee!" Rory said, in the silence. "Do . . . do you think he meant it?"

"Naw," said his father. "He's just mad."

"Nice going, Tank," the waiter beamed. "I thought we had a real mess of trouble on our hands for a minute. Say, you oughta take up wrestling on TV. Make yourself a lot of money."

"I'm not looking for any medals for taking a knife off an old man," Tank Millard said sarcastically. "All right, Rory, let's go. We're late. Steve! I want a word with you outside."

"Yeah, Boss." Wirkowski stood a good six inches taller than Rory's father, but he grabbed his parka and followed obediently. At the door Millard had an afterthought. "Chub, send me the bill for the broken dishes, okay?" Then the three stepped outside and the cold stabbed their faces.

"Now, Steve,"—Tank Millard's words came back in puffs of frozen breath—"you know how I feel about fighting in a place like that. I won't stand for it. This is the last time. Understand?"

"Yeah," Wirkowski said reluctantly.

"If you have to fight, take it out in the alley. But you shouldn't have to fight. Old Cornflakes was partly right. We're the outsiders up here. If we go throwing our weight around, it looks bad for us, for the company, for the whole business."

"He started it," Wirkowski said stubbornly.

"I'm sure he did. He's a mean, unreasonable, cantankerous old mountain goat. Last year we were drilling over to the east of here and he was always yakking at us."

"Cornflakes: that's a funny name," said Rory.

"Everybody calls him that. I guess he has a real name but I don't know what it is."

"How'd he get called 'Cornflakes'?"

"It goes away back to when he was younger. He runs a trapline, just over the boundary in the Territories. One winter he got a lot of furs, got a good price for them, and went into Edmonton to get drunk. He rented the whole floor of a little hotel, got in a bunch of cronies and had a party. Along about the third day he wanted to show a city guy how to snowshoe. So he sent out for cornflakes. Must have bought four or five hundred boxes. Dumped them all out in the corridor and snowshoed up and down that hall all day."

"He's crazy," Wirkowski grunted.

"He might be a little off his rocker," agreed Rory's father. "When you live alone all the time the way he does, you get that way. But we've never bothered him and I hope he'll leave us alone. I've got enough to do without fighting trappers."

They were at the little frame shack that served as the Fort Mackenzie base for WestCan Oil. Inside, it was smoky and crowded. Rory's father glanced round the room and said, "Well, it looks as though the advance party got here. Hello, Dutch. Sorry I'm late. Have you started yet?"

"Waited for you," said Dutch Kruger, the assistant tool-push. He was a broad, slow-moving red-faced man with bleached eyebrows and eyes the colour of faded blue jeans. "Okay boys, let's settle down."

"Hang on one more minute, Dutch, I want a word with Lefebvre," Rory's father said. "Hi, René."

"How are you, Tank?" He was a slim little man with glossy black hair that came down in long sideburns. His thin moustache was neatly trimmed and his blue-black beard fresh-shaven. He had on a clean red shirt under his parka. Even his fingernails were clean. His white smile lit up his whole face. Rory liked him right away.

"I want you to meet the boy," said Tank Millard. "Rory, this is René Lefebvre. He's the cook. You'll be working with him."

"Hello, Rory," said Lefebvre and stuck out his hand.

"You remember what I said, René," Rory's father went on. "He'll work a full shift, same as anybody else would, and he'll attend to his lessons in between. Okay?"

"Okay." Lefebvre winked. "We'll do fine. Your first trip to a camp, eh, Rory? Dutch, what do we call this wildcat?"

"Huh?"

"What's the name? What's it called in the records?"

"Well, in the records it's WestCan Mackenzie Number One."

"Who cares about records!" Lefebvre said. "This one we will call Rory's Wildcat."

Dutch Kruger grinned and said nothing. Tank Millard shrugged.

"Call it what you like, around camp. All right, boys, gather round." He began to review the plans: the order in which the trucks would move out, who would ride in each, how they would lay out the camp on arrival. Rory sat back in a corner, watching, listening. Was it one of these men who had been in the restaurant less than an hour ago, taking instructions from that oil scout? Maybe it was a wild idea, but he couldn't help looking them over, sizing them up, wondering.

There was Oscar Reason, the geologist his father had mentioned. He stood off by himself in the opposite corner, a sulky-looking man with a pale soft-looking face. Not very friendly—he only spoke when he was spoken to—but he didn't look as though he needed money. He had a big flashy ring on his left hand, and while most of the other men wore parkas and jeans, Reason wore an expensive-looking snowmobile suit.

There was Wirkowski, the one who had been in the fight with old Cornflakes. He was leaning against the wall, bigger than all the rest, still scowling. He was tough, no doubt about it. Rory didn't trust him. Suppose—Rory caught his breath at the thought—that Wirkowski was the one. Yes, it was possible. He *could* have gone out the back door, then sneaked in again. Wirkowski was certainly a man to watch. His eyes, shifting across the room, caught Rory's. He did not smile or wink or nod, just stared. Rory hastily looked away.

He studied the others: Jim Garnett, big with long blond curly hair and beard. He seemed to do a lot of talking and laughing and the others seemed to like him: Harvey Clay, who held himself so straight that he reminded Rory of pictures of the Duke of Edinburgh—except that the Duke never wore thick glasses or overalls.

There were others, but suddenly Rory realized that he was so tired he ached, and so hungry that he felt a little faint. It was six-thirty and he'd had only a sandwich, a sundae, and a hot chocolate since morning. With a sigh of relief he heard his father say, "That's it. See you all at a quarter to six in the morning."

The men drifted away, most of them toward the restaurant. Tank Millard stayed behind for a word with Dutch Kruger, his assistant. Lefebvre gave Rory a pat on the shoulder and said, "See you tomorrow." Clay, the straight-backed man, stopped and told Rory, "I hear you're going to study, up at the camp. Maybe I can give you a hand with the books. Be good practice for me: I'm going back to university one day soon."

"Gee, thanks." At least some people were friendly. Maybe it wouldn't be so bad after all. But Wirkowski brushed past him without a word.

At the restaurant they had steak and mashed potatoes and pie. His father was lost in thought. Rory didn't care; he almost fell asleep over the last bite. He looked around once for Wirkowski but the big man had vanished. Then Rory followed his father through the icy darkness to the little hotel, their feet squeaking through the brittle snow.

The next thing he knew his father was shaking him awake.

"Five o'clock. Dress warm." It was still black outside and the frost had painted a fancy jungle of white ferns and palm trees on the window. Rory blinked the sleep away and pulled on thick woollen underwear, heavy socks, shirt, nylon pants, fleece-lined flight boots. He splashed water on his face, shoved parka, woollen toque and mittens under his arm, and went downstairs. The little hotel coffee shop had opened two hours earlier than usual, as a favour to WestCan's crew. Rory gulped a bowl of porridge, two fried eggs, fruit juice, milk, and toast. Then Tank Millard stood up and the roomful of men filed out after him.

Outdoors, the cold ran down Rory's throat into his lungs and took his breath away. It was thirty below zero, somebody said. In the vacant lot behind the WestCan office the truckers had left their motors running all night so that they would not freeze up. It was an eerie sight. They stood in rows, great growling monsters with plumes of diesel oil exhaust coming from the pipes that stuck up in the air behind the drivers' cabs. They were loaded with tons of drill pipe, parts of the steel derrick, great engines to drive the drill, and the green plywood trailers set on wooden platforms that would be homes for the crew.

Rory's father climbed into the cab of the first truck and waved the driver on. Rory and René Lefebvre went into the next one, beside a tobacco-chewing driver named Dino. Dino said, "Let's roll," and shifted into the first of the truck's sixteen gears. The twenty-ton load crunched slowly away.

The few early morning lights of Fort Mackenzie fell behind as they turned out onto the Mackenzie Highway. Behind, Rory could hear the growl of other trucks. He knew that the whole WestCan cavalcade was winding like a caterpillar toward the Northwest Territories. Daylight was still hours away. The great adventure was on. Somewhere ahead was the site of Rory's wildcat.

Rory remembered what his father had said yesterday: that no scout back in the bush could see into their rig because of the canvas covers to keep out the cold. But his father hadn't reckoned on one thing—a spy *inside* camp as well as out.

And if Rory's hunch was right, there *was* a second spy, maybe even in this caravan.

4

Sabotage

"Where're we going?" Lefebvre said.

"Don't know, exactly," the driver said through his tobacco. "Tank knows and Kruger knows and the bull-dozer crews that cut the sideroad into the campside know, but they ain't been broadcasting the word around town."

"Hope we stay on this road a while longer," said Lefebvre.

"You and me both. Those bush roads are murder. I broke an axle last year."

They fell silent. Rory slouched down warmly between them, lulled by the drone of the big motor and the soft glow of lights from the dashboard. They had been on the road two hours, but morning was still only a smudge of grey light in the east. They were making good time over the snow-caked highway, through gently rolling hills covered with poplar, spruce and jackpine. Rory remembered, too, from the plane ride yesterday, that the land was full of frozen lakes. It was all white, black, and grey, a cold, empty-looking country.

He began to feel sorry for himself again. He was going into the wilderness to live with men he didn't know. His father was just as distant as ever. There were no other kids to play with. There wouldn't be enough time for studying and he'd probably flunk his year. And on top of everything else, somewhere around there was probably a desperate character, maybe even on this rig. If he could only find out for sure. Then if the man was spying on WestCan, Rory would trap him and his father would be pleased and . . .

Suddenly Rory noticed something that he had discovered long ago: that if a boy—even a boy as big as he was now—scrunched down and was quiet and closed his eyes, grownups forgot he was there. They also forgot to wink and nudge him in the ribs and make dumb jokes that

23

no boy would ever laugh at except to be polite. In fact, they acted like grownups, and said all kinds of interesting things. It was happening now.

"I hear Tank put the arm on somebody in the restaurant last night," Dino was saying.

"Yes. The old trapper, Cornflakes. He pulled a knife on Wirkowski."

"I sure wouldn't jump that old bandit if he was waving a knife around. He looks scrawny but I've seen him fight. He's as tough as my boot."

"Tank is not afraid of many things," Lefebvre said quietly.

"He did pretty good in the Korean War, they say."

"Yes. He was working in the States when the war broke out. Joined the U.S. Army. Ended up in charge of a tank outfit."

"That where he got the nickname?"

Lefebvre nodded.

"The newspapers, y'know. Tank and his bunch cracked through an enemy line, sprung loose an infantry unit that was trapped. Tank got a medal and some newspaper guy pinned the name on him."

"Jeez," said Dino, "if Tank was in Korea he's no spring chicken. A guy his age should have a nice soft office job."

"He could get a good office job with this company if he wanted it," Lefebvre said. "He doesn't want it. He likes this life. He *loves* it. He's been all over Canada, the States, the North Sea. Whenever they have a tough one to drill, they send for Tank Millard."

"Beats me," Dino said. "I sure wouldn't follow these rigs if I didn't need the money."

"Nobody but Tank would," said Lefebvre. "Look at me: I do it 'cause I have to support my kids."

"I didn't know you had kids."

"Have I got kids! Man, I was married two times!"

Dino spat hard out the window. "You sure are a bear for punishment, René."

"Well, somehow it just happened. First time in Montreal, my poor wife died. She was a lovely girl. Left me with three little ones. Then I moved to St. Boniface, got

24

married again. Oh, she was a beauty, that one. Jacqueline! Like a movie star. Like that, what's her name, Geneviève Bujold . . ." Lefebvre's voice trailed off.

"Well." Dino cleared his throat. "Uh, I hope nothing bad happened to *her*?"

"Oh no. She run off with another man, is all. Too bad. She left me with four more kids."

"Jeez! Well, I guess you learned your lesson."

"I dunno, Dino. I wouldn't mind getting married again. I am not so old and not bad to look at and I can cook better'n most women. But my church don't let me get a divorce. So I got a housekeeper to mind the kids and I got to pay her five hundred dollars a month and give her room and board and the kids need shoes and school books and, man, you ought to see those kids *eat*!"

The driver chuckled.

"Well, anybody gets married more'n once, he deserves all the trouble he gets. Me, I'm not even gonna make that mistake once, y'know."

"Doesn't matter," said Lefebvre. "You need money, eh? Married or single, seven kids or none, it doesn't matter. Look at Garnett."

"What about him?"

"Gambles. Dice, cards: you name it, Garnett plays it. Sometimes he wins, more times he loses. He's a bachelor but he's always broke."

"Garnett . . . Jim Garnett," the driver said thoughtfully. "Wasn't he mixed up in some kind of scandal a few years back?"

Rory, who had almost fallen asleep—the conversation about marriage was pretty boring—came wide awake in an instant. Scandal?

"Sure," Lefebvre was saying. "Same old thing. Trouble with money. He was fullback for one of those pro football teams in the States. Fine player. Then the big scandal. Somebody claimed that Garnett took a bribe. Remember?"

"Yeah, I think so. He got kicked out of football, right?"

"That's right. They never proved about the bribe but he sure had been betting on the games. Same as now: Garnett is always looking for money."

So Garnett needs money, always, Rory thought. Could

25

he use ten thousand dollars so badly he would spy on his boss's rig? But Lefebvre was not finished.

"Then there is Clay."

"The young guy who carries his nose up in the air? What's his problem?"

"Money. He's got a big plan. He's going back to university and be a lawyer and then he's going into politics. He's got it all mapped out. I never see such ambition. But he needs money."

Lefebvre yawned noisily, then went on. "Even Oscar Reason . . ."

"Aw, come on, René, that guy is made of money!"

"No, that is not true. I tell you a little secret about him, but don't tell the rest of the boys. Oscar has got a wife that spends it faster than he makes it. She came from a rich family, y'know, and she sure knows how to spend. They have the big house in Edmonton and the big car and they belong to the country club. I give you an example: you know that big ring Oscar wears? It's a real diamond, Dino. He say to me the other day, 'The missus gave it to me for a Christmas present. It is real nice but it cost *me* three thousand dollars.' And he say, 'René, I need money so bad I feel like robbing a bank.' No, Dino, you never can tell just by looking. Everybody needs money. So here we are in this cold weather, five hundred miles from our families, all after money, eh? It's a funny life."

The names were tumbling over and over in Rory's head. Oscar Reason: yes, nobody was in a better position to get information than Oscar. He could get the core samples, everything. Garnett had a reason, too, and so did Clay. And nobody had even mentioned Wirkowski. Even Lefebvre himself, with seven children, could use ten thousand dollars. What a mess. And for that matter, it might not be any of them: Rory was only guessing that the spy was on their crew.

Dino shifted gears three times and coaxed the truck up a steep hill. "How come you know so much about everybody, René? Man, the way you hear everybody's troubles, you oughta be a priest."

Lefebvre shrugged. "They talk at meals. They talk and play cards at night and I listen. I am interested. I like

26

people." He began to sing a little tune, "Jolie Jacqueline."

"Is that Jolly Jacqueline the one who was your second wife, René?" Rory asked, and instantly realized he had given himself away. Dino bellowed with laughter.

"You old sonofagun, you were listening all the time," said Lefebvre cheerfully. "Well, the song could be about my Jacqueline. It's *jolie,* Rory, not jolly. That means 'pretty' in French. And she was a lovely girl, Rory. Like a movie star."

"Hey, there's the sideroad, off to the left," Dino interrupted. Five hundred yards ahead, the first truck was moving off into the bush. At the turn-off, Dutch Kruger was parked in a jeep to guide the WestCan caravan onto the trail.

"Here we go on the roller coaster," Dino said. "Hold on to your seats, there is no admission charge."

It was a very bad road. It had been carved out by a bulldozer and the trees were cleared away, true enough. But the trail was a series of frozen hummocks and even at a crawl it almost shook a man's teeth loose. It put an end to conversation, except for the occasional oath from Dino, when the truck dropped into a pot-hole with a sickening thud.

Suddenly Rory cried, "Look, they've stopped."

The first truck had halted at the foot of a hill. As they drew near, they saw the driver and Tank Millard climb down and open the hood. A cloud of steam rose from inside.

Dino pulled up and they climbed down and hurried over to Tank Millard's side.

"Trouble?"

"Radiator's heating up. Looks like we sprung a leak in the hose."

The driver pulled his head out of the steam and looked angrily at the others. "It didn't just spring a leak, Tank. Somebody punched a hole in it!"

27

5

Four Indians

"Punched a hole in it!" Tank Millard repeated. "Now who the devil'd do a thing like that?"

"See for yourself," said the driver. "See? If it was an ordinary leak it'd be cracked, right? But this is brand new hose with three neat little holes in it. Somebody's stuck it with something sharp." He pointed to the rubber hose that connected the radiator to the engine. A small plume of steam was still rising from tiny punctures in the hose. The driver spat angrily in the snow.

"Pretty smart: just little holes, so it wouldn't run out fast. But big enough so that when we got going and the water pressure built up, then it started to leak out. It took this long for me to lose enough water for the engine to heat up."

"Now who the devil?" Rory's father said again. Then he looked at the others. "Cornflakes! That rotten old . . . If I thought it was him I'd nail his old hide to his cabin door!"

"Aw, why would stupid Cornflakes do a thing like this?" Dino said. "If he really wanted to stop us, he'd've put sugar in the gas tank or slashed the tires."

"No, this is how that old man's mind works," said Rory's father. "See, I don't think he really wants to do us much harm. And he sure didn't want anything to happen in town, 'cause he knew we'd jump him. No, he just wants to pester us. And he'd want to do it like this, out on the road, where we'd have no chance to find the guy who did it."

"Maybe you're right." Dino nodded. "He could have slipped the hood up and stuck a spike into this hose in half a minute, while the watchman was having coffee."

"That's another reason I'm guessing it was him," Tank Millard said. "He can move as quiet as a timber wolf. Dammit! I wish I could prove it. Well, have you got a spare hose, Bob?"

"Nope," his driver said. "But I can patch this if you find me a good big roll of friction tape."

"Dino," said Tank Millard, "get on your CB radio. Call Kruger to bring us a roll of tape. And hurry! We're losing time and we've still got fifteen miles to do."

Dino hurried into the cab of his truck. Other WestCan trucks were pulled up in a line, waiting. Rory walked back along the road a little way, thinking, well, if old Cornflakes wanted to slow us down, he sure did a neat job.

Then he had another thought. Maybe it wasn't Cornflakes who had sabotaged the truck! Maybe it was one of those two men in the restaurant. Only why would they do a thing like this, if what they really wanted was to spy on the rig? He walked up and down the roadside for a while, trying to make something out of that idea, until the cold began to bite through his clothes. Boy, this Northwest Territories was sure colder than Edmonton, and Edmonton wasn't exactly Florida.

He was about to climb back into Dino's truck when he saw them: four figures standing silently at the end of the trees, beside the road.

"Hey, René, look!" Rory hissed. "Indians!"

They were an old man, another about the age of Rory's father, a boy about Rory's size and a girl slightly smaller. They stood watching but not moving or speaking. The old man was dressed in caribou parka with wolf fur trim; the others wore clothes much like Rory's. They were not quite like the Indians Rory remembered from school books. Their faces were brown, all right, but they looked more like Eskimos or—what were those people he'd studied about last year?—Mongolians, that was it.

"Look like Dogribs," said Tank Millard.

"Dogribs?" said the truck driver. "I thought all the native people around here were Slavey or Loucheux."

"Mostly. But there's this small tribe around Yellowknife and Fort Rae. Quite rare, really, this is the only place on earth you'll meet them. There's a little of the Asiatic in their looks. They used to hunt and trap and roam around. Now, I dunno."

The four Dogribs moved slowly toward the truck.

"Hello," said Tank Millard.

The younger man nodded. "Hi. You guys with an oil company?"

"Uh-huh. You hunting?"

The Dogrib shrugged. "My ole man likes to look for fox now 'n' then so we came out with the Skidoo." He jerked his head toward a snowmobile half-hidden in the bush. "But there's not much fox this year. Don't much like huntin', myself. Got a cigarette?"

The truck driver fished out a packet and offered it. The two Dogrib men nodded their thanks, accepted lights, took long puffs and smiled.

"Got any jobs?" the young one said. "Not much work in Yellowknife this winter."

"What can you do?" Millard asked.

"Odd jobs. Fix things. I can fix motors."

"Come see me after we get the rig up. My crew is all hired but maybe I can find you something."

The children had drifted to one side. The two young Dogribs stood close together, staring silently at Rory. Rory stared back. Now that he was over his surprise, it was kind of nice to see other kids again. The girl had a merry, impish face that looked as though it would burst into laughter if someone threw a secret switch. She had dark eyelashes and she was, Rory thought, rather pretty.

Her brother—at least, he probably was her brother—had coarse black hair that fell in his face and shrewd black eyes. He was chewing bubble-gum. Still watching Rory, he blew a large pink bubble, sucked it in, suddenly said, "My name's Sammy Football," and blew another.

"You speak English!" blurted Rory.

Sammy Football let out a disgusted sigh that shattered his bubble-gum with a little splat. He licked it back into his mouth and began chewing again. "Boy, are you ever weird. 'Course I speak English. What'd you think I was, a Russian or something?"

"Well, I didn't know . . . well, I'm Rory. Rory Millard."

"That's a funny name. I never heard of anybody called Rory."

"Well," Rory said, a little indignantly, "I never heard of anybody called Football, either. Football's a game."

Sammy changed the subject. He pointed a thumb over his shoulder.

"That's Annie, my sister."

"Hello," said Rory.

Annie flicked him a glance and a shy smile.

"And that's my ole man, and *his* ole man," Sammy continued, pointing to the other Dogribs. "You got an ole man too?"

"That's my father that your father was talking to." Rory hesitated, then couldn't resist adding, "My dad's the boss of the whole oil rig and all the men."

Sammy Football snapped his bubble-gum again.

"My ole man can fix trucks. And my ole granpa used to be the best hunter between here and Aklavik. Caribou, fox, he can catch anything. Once"——Sammy chewed furiously and squinted at the sky—". . . once he tracked a wolf a whole day. And killed it with a stick."

"Half a day," Annie said suddenly. "And he used a gun."

"It was more'n half a day," argued Sammy. "It was afternoon anyway, when he got it." He looked back at Rory with a tired expression. "She thinks she's so smart because she's a year younger'n me and in the same grade."

"You go to school?"

"Sometimes. Sometimes me 'n granpa go hunting. Sometimes I just stay home."

"That where you learned English?"

"Uh-huh. And from TV and comic books."

"You've got *TV*?"

Sammy groaned and slapped his forehead.

"You gotta be kidding! You think we're savages or something? Yeah, we got TV, out of Yellowknife."

"Do you ever watch 'Star Trek'?"

"I like 'Buck Rogers' better." Sammy gave an ear splitting imitation of a rocket ship leaving for outer space. "And I like all the comic books."

"You know what teacher says," Annie interrupted. "If you read those comic books all the time, your brain'll turn to porridge."

"Yeah, but she says I'm better'n you at math, too. She says I'm the best in fractions she ever seen."

"Saw," corrected Annie. Sammy sighed noisily and rolled his eyes.

"I don't like fractions much, either." Rory looked sympathetically at Annie. "I hate math. I'm better in composition. I bet you are too." Annie blushed and said nothing.

"Your truck broke down, hey?" said Sammy. "I'm gonna be a truck driver and a mechanic when I grow up. Bet I'll be able to fix it quicker'n you guys are doing."

Rory suddenly felt an awful urge to impress Sammy Football.

"It didn't just break down. Somebody sabotaged it!" He lowered his voice. "I think there's a spy around here some place."

"Yeah?" Sammy stopped chewing.

Rory plunged on, "Yes, I heard two men talking about spying on us, back in Fort Mackenzie. I think they're going to steal information from my father's oil rig. I haven't told anybody but you yet."

"Wow!" Sammy Football's eyes grew wide.

"If they want to steal information from you, how come they're wasting time breaking down your truck?" Annie said suddenly.

Rory looked at Annie for a while. That was the question that had been bothering him. He began to get the uneasy feeling that Annie was a lot smarter than he'd figured at first, and a whole lot smarter than Sammy. Finally he said, "Well, I've read a lot of books about spies. And sometimes spies do things like this to throw you off their trail. They figure you'll blame somebody else and then they can keep on sneaking around, doing their spying and stealing."

"Well, who do the spies want to put the blame on?" demanded Annie.

This Annie was a thinker, all right. Still, she was nice about it, not smart-alecky. Rory frowned and put a finger to his lips. The men were standing around waiting for the tape and idly looking over at Rory and the two young Indians.

Rory whispered, "Old Cornflakes. My father and the

others think he made our truck break down. And I bet that's exactly what the spy wants them to think."

"Cornflakes? He's that trapper," Sammy said. "He's got a cabin way over past our place."

"That's the one," said Rory. "He fought with one of our men last night and he threatened us. But I'll bet he didn't do this."

"Why not?" said Annie. "Maybe he's one of the spies."

"Well," Rory said, "well, I don't think he is." Darn that Annie! Maybe she was right. The oil scout hadn't said, "You'll be on the rig." He'd said, "You'll be handy to everything." That could mean Cornflakes!

He'd thought of the possibility of Cornflakes being the oil scout, though the voice didn't sound right. But maybe Cornflakes wasn't the oil scout. Maybe he was the second man in the restaurant, the one whose voice he hadn't heard.

Just then the jeep bounced over a hummock with Dutch Kruger at the wheel. He sprang out with a roll of heavy black tape.

"More trouble, back down the road, Tank," he said. "Couple more trucks had to stop. Losing water, same as this one. Same reason."

Tank Millard strode away a few steps, his fists rammed in his parka pockets. He came back, while the truck driver named Bob wound tape round the hose. "Okay boys, let's go. We've lost an hour already."

"I'll see you at camp one of these days," Sammy whispered. "Maybe we can help you track those spies. I'm a good tracker. I'm about the best between here and Aklavik."

"Granpa's better," said Annie.

Sammy ignored her. "See you," he repeated.

"You bet," said Rory. He swung into the cab beside Dino and waved. Then the cavalcade growled into gear and on down the road.

"Cheer up," said Dino. "Fifteen more miles and we'll be there, if the springs hold out."

"They will hold out longer than my back," Lefebvre groaned.

Rory settled down in the warmth from the heater. Fifteen more miles. Then the rig would go up. Then, sooner or later, the spy would have to make his move. Who could it be? Cornflakes, Wirkowski, Clay, Garnett, Reason, Lefebvre? Or somebody else? Rory sighed and closed his eyes. Well, I always liked mysteries, he thought, and now I'm in the middle of a real one. Boy, am I ever!

6

Cornflakes's Cabin

It was afternoon when the trucks crawled into the campsite. There had been no more breakdowns, but the crew was tired, cold, hungry and out of sorts. Now, as they pulled into the clearing in the woods, Rory thought it was the loneliest place on earth. WestCan's bulldozers had cleared a large, lopsided square out of the jackpine and spruce. That was all: nothing else. And this was to be home for weeks, months even.

But suddenly it began to look like home. Quickly the crew unloaded the diesel trailer that would generate electricity for the whole camp; kitchen and dining trailers; sleeping trailers; an office trailer with two beds for Millard and Kruger, desks, filing cabinets, a two-way radio for talking to incoming aircraft and a regular push-button telephone connected to the outside world by satellite through a portable dish-shaped antenna set up outdoors.

There was a recreation trailer with pool table, shuffle board, TV, movie screen and projector, cribbage board, magazines and card tables. And there was a washroom with gleaming basins, showers and flush toilets.

The sleek metal trailers, with thick foam insulation between the walls and imitation wood panelling on the inside, were cleverly made to lock together, so that the electrical wiring and oil heating system ran right through camp. They were fitted together in a T-shape—kitchen and dining trailers, office, washroom and rec trailers all along the top of the T, sleeping trailers in a double row down the base of the T with a central hall between. Once indoors, the men could eat, sleep and play without ever stepping out into the bitter cold. It was rather like a little village, Rory thought.

Lunch that day was a hasty affair of coffee and sandwiches that had been packed the night before. Then, while the crew went on setting up camp, Lefebvre said cheerfully, "Now Rory, you and I have to work for a living."

They unpacked the tin plates, china mugs, knives, forks and spoons. Lefebvre set out an enormous heap of frozen steaks to thaw for supper. Then, while Lefebvre fired up the propane gas stove and made huge salads, Rory set out plates and clusters of utensils, found salt and pepper, bread and butter, jam and pickles. He punctured cans of fruit juice, ready to pour. He filled pitchers with milk.

"You sure feed them, René. I thought people in bush camps just ate beans and bacon and stuff."

"The company buys the best and I'm the best cook there is," Lefebvre said matter-of-factly. He began to flip steaks into a pan. "Look at that meat: two inches thick! Some of these boys never ate better in their lives."

After a while he slipped a small steak on a plate with some sliced tomatoes and mashed potatoes.

"Here." He motioned Rory to a stool at a corner of the small kitchen table. "Eat this, right now. I bet you're hungry."

Rory *was* hungry. Something about eating always cheered him up and he'd never tasted anything quite so good as this.

"Boy, can you ever cook, René!"

Lefebvre beamed.

"Wait'll you try my blueberry pie. Ah, I don't know why that Jacqueline left me, a man who can cook as good as me. Well, here come the men."

And they came, in out of the dark and the criss-cross beams of the truck headlights. It had been dark nearly two hours now, although it was only six o'clock. They filed past the kitchen and loaded their plates, cafeteria style, then sat at tables that folded out from the walls of the dining trailer. Rory worked furiously, re-filling milk pitchers, coffee urn, steak tray, salad bowls. And in the kitchen Lefebvre moved in his white apron through magnificent clouds of smoke, magically producing more steaks and humming "Jolie Jacqueline" off key.

Finally the last man was fed. Rory sat down wearily on his stool. There hadn't been much time to think about the spy, and anyway, since there was no information for a spy to steal yet, Rory couldn't get very concerned. The crew carried their dishes out to the kitchen and then Garnett said, "Who feels like a little blackjack?"

Oscar Reason shook his head and left. Wirkowski said gruffly, "For half an hour, maybe." Clay asked, "You playing for money?"

"Why not?" said Garnett. "You might make your fortune."

Clay grunted. "I haven't noticed you making any fortune."

"I might any day now." Garnett grinned.

"I can find better ways to make money than at cards."

"You two gonna play or argue?" demanded Wirkowski. So they found a deck of cards and gathered in the rec trailer.

As Rory helped Lefebvre with the dishes, he wondered, sleepily, what Clay meant by "better ways to make money." His father looked in and said to Rory, "How's it going?" with an absent look on his face, then went out again. It was plain that he had other things on his mind.

Rory was ready for bed. He found the trailer he was to share with Lefebvre. It was a neat little place with a table, reading lamp, two chairs and two beds with blankets and clean white sheets. He burrowed in. He remembered sleepily that this was Monday, January 10, and that he'd better get at those books tomorrow. Then he was asleep.

The days that followed were a blur. By now the full crew had arrived from Edmonton and Peace River, shuttled in aboard a Twin Otter to a little gravel airstrip near the rig. Among them was Lefebvre's assistant cook to help feed forty men—a skinny little man, as silent as his boss was talkative.

But Rory was as busy as ever, washing dishes and cleaning up the dining trailer after meals. He was up at six each morning and in the kitchen soon after. There, his chores lasted until nine. Then back to the trailer where he studied until eleven. Then it was time to help during the noon meal and tidy up afterward. By one-thirty he was free again until half-past five. Time to study some more, then have a nap or a walk round the campsite before supper. By nine o'clock he was in bed, and glad of it.

The others were just as busy. In three days they had dug the "cellar" (a pit under the rig), put down the rig foundations, set up the diesel engines, assembled the derrick and spudded in. By Thursday, it stood, a network of steel, its head poking a hundred and twenty feet into the air, soaring above the treetops. At night, with lights glittering from its sides, it looked like part of a circus midway. Inside its framework, ninety-foot lengths of pipe were stacked on end. The engines were rumbling twenty-four hours a day, driving the drill bit deeper and deeper into the earth.

Rory remembered the oil scout's orders in the restaurant: "I want to know when they spud in . . ." According to that, the spy, whoever he was, ought to be getting a message out to the oil scout pretty soon. But try as he would, Rory saw no crewmen acting suspiciously and no signs of strangers around the camp. Could he have been wrong about the whole thing? Had the two men been talking about some other rig? Rory was heartily glad he hadn't told any of this to his father.

The WestCan men were on two twelve-hour shifts, right around the clock. They worked seven days a week, but after each two-week stint they were flown out for a two-week break, while another set of men replaced them. On Thursday Harvey Clay, who worked the day shift, poked his head into Rory's trailer after a coffee break.

"Hitting the books?" he said, wiping the steam from his glasses.

"I was trying to figure out the difference between a parallelogram and a trapezoid," Rory said. "I was about ready to quit."

"Don't quit. Otherwise you'll end up digging ditches or heaving drill pipe all your life. That's for suckers."

"But you're doing it!"

"Not for much longer." Clay winked and tapped his forehead. "The way to make money is to use your head, not your back. And that's what I aim to do. Give me a holler when you want your geometry checked."

He was gone before Rory could even say "Thanks." Rory sat staring blankly at the textbook. This was the sec-

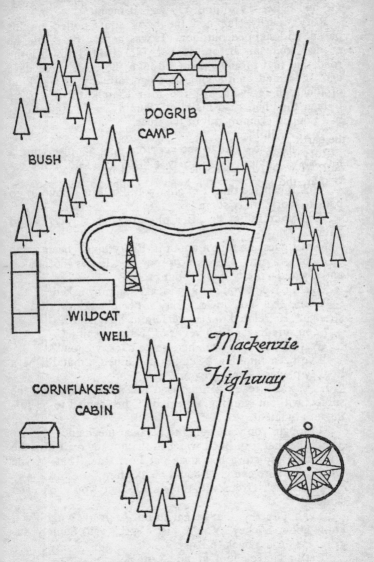

DOGRIB CAMP

BUSH

WILDCAT WELL

CORNFLAKES'S CABIN

Mackenzie Highway

ond time Clay had mentioned easy ways to make money. He had better try to find out what it meant.

Rory wearily slammed the book shut, pulled on his parka, and stepped outdoors. It was getting dark, but he needed some air before supper. He strolled toward the road that had brought them through the bush three days ago. It seemed such a long time ago, already. It was kind of lonely here, with just the men to talk to. Then, as though they had read his mind, Sammy and Annie Football popped grinning out of the trees.

"Well, hello!"

"My ole man came to see your ole man about getting a job, so we came over to see you," Sammy said, unnecessarily.

"Yes, I can see that. I'm glad you did. But I have to go back to work pretty soon."

"Did your father go after old Cornflakes yet?" asked Annie.

"No. I guess he forgot about it. Everything's been going all right. Anyway, there's no proof that it was Cornflakes and my dad's pretty fussy about proof."

"Well, haven't you got any ideas?" Sammy asked.

"Sure, I've got ideas. Clay's been talking kind of strange." He related the conversations he'd heard.

"You sure haven't got very far," Sammy sniffed.

"Well, we've only been here three days, y'know!"

"I've been thinking," Sammy continued, "that I'll be a hockey player when I grow up."

Rory was already getting used to Sammy changing the subject without warning, especially if he seemed to be losing an argument.

"I thought you were going to be a car mechanic?"

"I'll be that too. But I watched the hockey on TV in the Hudson's Bay store last spring at Fort Rae. That Wayne Gresky, he sure can go. I could be like him."

"His name's Gretzky," Annie said, "and you can't even skate."

"Yeah, Gretzky, that's what I said. Anyway, what d'you know about hockey? You're just a girl," said Sammy angrily. He turned back to Rory.

"Let's go have a look at old Cornflakes tomorrow."

"Huh?"

"Let's go over to his cabin and see what he's up to. know where it is."

"I think we'd better leave that old guy alone. He's mean. You should have seen the way he swung his knife back in that restaurant."

"We won't let him see us. We'll sneak up, same as we'd sneak up on a caribou. I'm real good at it."

"But I have to study."

"Couldn't you get the afternoon off?" Annie begged. "We could go right after lunch and be back in time for you to go to work."

"If you can walk as fast as we can," added Sammy.

"I can walk as fast as you any day," Rory said. "I s'pose I could take tomorrow afternoon off, if I made up for it on Saturday. Okay, see you right after lunch."

"Blast off," Sammy said, and made a noise like a space ship as he and Annie disappeared into the bush.

The Footballs appeared promptly at one-thirty the next afternoon.

"How do you always know what time it is?" Rory asked.

Sammy grinned mischievously. "I tell time by the sun. Can't you?"

"Well, what do you do on cloudy days?"

Annie giggled. "He looks at his wristwatch—same as he does on sunny days!"

"You're lucky you don't have a smart-aleck sister," grumbled Sammy, and led the way into the bush.

It was heavy walking in places, where the snow had drifted among the trees, but Sammy Football led the way, breaking a path and following rabbit and fox trails when he could. Annie came second and Rory brought up the rear. Even so, with the others breaking trail for him, he was almost exhausted when they stopped for a rest after an hour.

"You walk pretty good for a city kid," said Sammy.

Rory tried hard not to show that he was out of breath. One way was to use short words. "Much farther?"

"About a half-hour." They pushed on and suddenly Sammy raised a warning hand. Through the trees Rory saw

43

a cabin, a small ordinary-looking one at the side of a hill. They crept forward, not too close, and dropped to their stomachs to watch. There was smoke coming from the chimney, but no one came out.

"Let's get out of here," Annie whispered.

"Wait a minute," Sammy said. "Let's see if he comes out."

"See if who comes out?" a voice growled behind them.

They whirled round. There, not ten steps away, was old Cornflakes himself. He had a pair of empty traps over his shoulder and a rifle in his hand. He was on snowshoes and he had slipped up behind them as silently as a fox.

In a flash the Footballs were on their feet and darting into the bush. But Rory, his legs tired and trembling from the long walk, stumbled and fell on his face. He tried to get up again but it was too late. The trapper was standing right over him, rifle in hand.

7

The Scout Turns Up

Old Cornflakes was a lot bigger than Rory remembered, especially when you were on the ground looking up at him. Back in Fort Mackenzie he'd seemed short compared to Wirkowski and skinny compared to Rory's father. But now Rory could see that the trapper was tall and tough, and if he was old he sure didn't act like it. He had a two-day stubble of beard and he was scowling down at Rory as though he couldn't make up his mind whether or not to skin him like a muskrat.

"What are you doing around here, ya nosy little brat?" he snapped.

"Just . . . just looking."

"How long you been here? Did you see anything?"

"Noth-nothing, Mister Cornflakes."

"Oh, you know my name, huh? Who are you?"

"My name's Rory."

"Rory what? You a Dogrib? You don't look like an Indian."

"No. My friends are Dogribs."

"Where'd they go?" The trapper looked around. There was no sign of the Footballs. "Hey! You Indian kids! I know you're there. Come on out quick or I'll make your friend into a pelt."

There was silence. Then slowly, timidly, Sammy and Annie edged out of the bush. Rory knew they were as scared as he was, but Annie said bravely, "You let Rory go!"

"Shut up! C'mere and sit down. And don't anybody try to get away. I can outrun the lot of you."

Cornflakes tossed his traps at the foot of a tree, leaned his rifle against the trunk and fumbled in an inner pocket, watching them all the time.

"Snoopy kids!" He brought out a plug of chewing tobacco. "I know the two of you are Dogribs. But you . . ."

He stared at Rory. "I don't know you. Where you from? No lies, now!"

"I'm . . . I'm from the WestCan drill rig," Rory said reluctantly and then his voice faded away into nothing, for Cornflakes had pulled out that long wicked-looking hunting knife. The trapper glared at him, knife in hand.

"You're one of those stinkin' drillers! What's your name again?"

"Rory . . . uh . . . Millard."

"MILLARD! You're the toolpush's kid!"

Rory nodded miserably.

"I oughta notch your ears." The trapper fingered the knife and looked long and hard at Rory, but after a while he merely cut a chew from the plug of tobacco and popped it into his mouth. "Did your old man send you here to snoop?"

"No! No, he doesn't even know we're here." Right away, Rory wished he hadn't admitted that.

"He doesn't, eh? Well, now, that's interesting." Cornflakes munched juicily on the tobacco and seemed to be thinking. "How'd you find my cabin and how'd you know my name?"

"Sammy lives around here," Rory said. Sammy was strangely quiet. Rory went on, "And I saw you in the restaurant in Fort Mackenzie last Sunday."

The trapper scowled at the memory. "Yeah. Well, I oughta keep you here, just to get even with your old man. But I don't pick on kids. You three just fan your tails out of here."

The old man wasn't going to hurt them. Rory suddenly felt brave. Suddenly—afterwards he wondered how he could have been so bold—he blurted, "Did you punch holes in our radiator hose?"

"Huh?" The trapper looked astonished.

"Somebody punched holes in the rad hoses of some of our trucks last Monday."

The trapper looked sharply at Rory. Was there a trace of a grin on his face? It was impossible to guess what the old man was thinking. Finally he said, "So what happened? Did all the water leak out?"

"Yes. And the engines heated up and we had to stop."

Cornflakes threw his head back and laughed, a great braying laugh that showed a ragged row of tobacco-stained teeth. "I bet your old man was fit to be tied! Wish I could've seen him!" But his face quickly sobered and he said, "Now listen, you three. There's things going on in this country that you'd better keep out of. I don't want you around here again, ever. Don't try to sneak up 'cause I'll find your tracks and I'll know. And don't you tell a soul you talked to me, you understand?"

They nodded.

"You'd better not forget. Because I'll know if you've been here and I'll find out if you've told." His voice lowered almost to a whisper. "And then I'll come in the night, quiet, and I'll get you when you sleep!" He rolled the hunting knife around in his hand until the flat of the blade rested in his palm. Then he gave it a sharp flip. It flew, end over end, fast and bright as a beam of light, and went *thunk* into a tree. It stuck there, quivering in the trunk before their frightened eyes. Cornflakes showed his dirty teeth again. *"Now git!"*

They shot out of the clearing, Sammy in the lead. For a long while they neither stopped nor spoke. Then they paused for wind, gazing fearfully over their shoulders.

"Wow!" said Sammy. "He's a mean one all right."

"See what I mean?" Rory nodded. "You know, I'm beginning to think you were right, Annie. Maybe he was the second one in the restaurant. Maybe he is going to spy on our rig."

"You going to tell your father?"

"No way! He might go after the old man and he wouldn't be able to prove anything. And then Cornflakes'd know I told. And then he'd come for me in the night. He'd get me, too. You notice the way he snuck up on us back there?"

Annie shivered and nodded. "Let's hurry," she urged. It was dark now. But Sammy led them safely back to camp and Rory slipped into his trailer unnoticed. He was quiet through dinner, and after his chores he went straight to bed, too tired even to dream.

He stayed quietly in his trailer at the books the next morning after breakfast, stopped for the lunch chores and then went back to his studies again. He was deep in an essay on Champlain when Lefebvre poked his head in the trailer door.

"Do me a favour, Rory? I can't leave the stove for more than a minute, so would you run over and ask your dad if he ordered something from Fort Mackenzie? Man here with a truck says he has some stuff for our rig."

"Okay." On the way out Rory glanced at a small truck pulled up near the kitchen trailer. The driver was leaning against it. He had on a parka with the hood pulled up and he wore dark glasses although the sun wasn't bright. Rory glimpsed a hard thin face with a stubble of beard, a mouth that turned down at the corners and a nose that looked as though it had once been broken.

Rory entered his father's trailer. Dutch Kruger was there alone, writing a drilling report.

"My dad around, Mr Kruger?"

"Why no, Rory. I thought you knew. He had to go to Mackenzie real early this morning. Should be back pretty soon though. What can I do for you?"

"Well, there's a man with a half-ton truck over at the kitchen trailer. He says he has some stuff for us. Lefebvre said to ask if we ordered it."

Dutch Kruger frowned with the effort of thinking.

"I don't think Tank ordered anything," he said. "What's this fellow got?"

"I don't know, exactly. Something for the rig, I think."

"Doesn't sound right. I'd better talk to him."

They strolled slowly to the kitchen trailer. Kruger did not like to be hurried. "How're the lessons going?"

"Pretty good."

"Well, you're doing fine in the kitchen. We're real pleased."

The half-ton truck was still there, but the driver was gone.

"Lefebvre," Kruger called. "Where's your delivery man?"

The cook stuck his head out the door.

"He wandered off toward the rig, Dutch."

"What the devil's he doing over there? We don't want any strangers over there. I don't care who they are."

48

Kruger moved more quickly now, with Rory at his heels.

"That's him." Rory pointed. "The one with dark glasses."

"You!" Kruger bellowed. "Driver! Come over here!"

The stranger sauntered back.

"What's all this about supplies?" demanded Kruger.

"It looks like I made a mistake," the stranger said apologetically. "Just call me stupid! I asked your boys over there if this is the North American rig and of course it isn't."

Rory stared sharply at the man. There was something about the voice.

"I don't know of any NA outfits around here," Kruger said.

"Well, I'd better get back to the truck and read my directions again," said the man. "Sorry to have troubled you."

"No trouble," said Kruger. The man turned away.

"No, wait!" Rory cried. Kruger and the man turned round in surprise. "He's the one! He's an oil scout, Mr Kruger! He came here to spy on us!"

8

A Hidden Threat?

There was a moment's silence. Some of the day shift men —Wirkowski, Clay and Garnett—heard Rory's cry and hurried over. Oscar Reason stopped on his way to his trailer and returned. The stranger stared at Rory, but when he spoke he sounded friendly enough.

"What are you talking about, kid? I'm a trucker."

Now they all turned to Rory.

"That's a pretty strong thing to accuse a man of, Rory," Clay said. "You sure you haven't made a mistake?"

"I'm sure," Rory said stubbornly. "He's the one."

"Sonny, I've never seen you before in my life. Now, I haven't got time for any more of this nonsense. I've got a long way to drive before dark."

"Hold on a minute." Dutch Kruger's mind was slowly grappling with the situation. "Rory, where did you see this man?"

"Well, I didn't actually see him."

"There, what'd I tell you!" snapped the man. "You guys better keep this kid locked up or his mouth'll get you into a lot of trouble. I'm leaving. So long."

"It *was* him," Rory said desperately. "I know his voice. He was talking to another man in the restaurant at Fort Mackenzie. Maybe even somebody from this camp. They were talking about spying on our rig."

"Somebody from this rig!" Dutch Kruger looked shocked.

"What'd the other one look like?" asked Garnett.

"I didn't get a look at either of them."

"Then how do you know the other one was from our rig?" Garnett asked.

"Well, I don't exactly. . . ."

"Did you hear his voice?"

"Well, no. But I know this one's voice. He was there."

"I think you'd better stick around a little while, mister, until the boss comes home," Kruger said.

"I've had enough of this!" The man's voice was getting mean and ugly, exactly the way Rory had heard it in the restaurant. "This crazy kid heard a couple of guys talking, he didn't see either one, now he says I'm one of them. And you're going to hold me here for that? I hope you're ready to go to court, mister, because if you don't let me go this minute, that's exactly where I'm gonna take you and your whole company."

"He's right, Dutch," Garnett nodded. "We can't even charge him with trespassing. He's a trucker on a legitimate errand and he just strayed into the wrong camp. We'll have to let him go."

"Well . . ." Dutch Kruger shrugged. "Okay, mister, beat it."

"Well, thanks a lot!" said the stranger sarcastically. Miserably, Rory watched him leap into his truck, gun the motor and roar across the snow-packed campsite toward the road. At the very edge of camp he suddenly slammed on his brakes and stopped inches from a jeep coming in. It was Rory's father.

Tank Millard climbed angrily from the jeep and snapped, "What the devil's the idea of driving like that inside my camp? You think this is a drag strip?"

"Sorry." The other man huddled in his parka and looked straight ahead. "I'm late. Trying to make up for lost time."

"Well, take it easy, or you'll get there on a stretcher." He turned to the jeep. "Back your truck up and let me through and you can go."

"Dad, wait!" Rory sprinted across the clearing. "He's an oil scout! He came here to spy on us!"

Tank Millard looked at Rory, then at the man in the truck. He walked closer, hands on hips, and stared.

"Well, well! Hello there, Mister Cody."

The man said nothing.

"You're right, Rory," his father said in a chilly voice. "He's an oil scout all right. Vic Cody. Old acquaintance of mine. How are you, Vic? Long time no see!"

"You got it all wrong, Millard," Cody said. "I quit the

52

scouting racket a long time back. I'm running this truck now, delivering out of Mackenzie. And I'd appreciate it if you'd move your jeep."

"Now, what's your hurry, Vic?" said Tank Millard in a hurt tone. "You're not a bit more sociable than you ever were. Climb down out of the cab a minute. Yeah, *climb down*! And take off the glasses and let me have a good look at you."

Cody sullenly did as he was told, keeping an eye on the growing circle of WestCan men around him.

"Guess I haven't seen you since Oklahoma. That was the time our geologist caught you snooping around and you beat him up, wasn't it? I didn't think you'd have the nerve to come around one of my rigs ever again."

"I don't want trouble with you, Millard. Just let me go about my business."

"Question is, what *is* your business these days?" Tank Millard said. "Rory, what do you know about this man?"

"I heard a man with a voice just like his in the restaurant at Mackenzie, last Monday while I was waiting for you. He said he was a scout and wanted information on somebody's oil rig."

"Did he say whose rig?"

"Well . . . no."

"Did you see him, or see who he was talking to?"

"No."

"There, Millard!" Cody stepped forward triumphantly and tapped Rory's father on the chest. "You haven't a thing to go on except this kid's imagination and that's pretty wild. You let me out of here this minute or I'll sic the Mounties on you the minute I do get back!"

"Keep your hands off me, Vic," Rory's father said icily. "Don't tempt me. I still owe you a punch in the mouth for that boy in Oklahoma!" He deliberately took a handful of Cody's parka, pulled the man forward and threw him back like a cork against his truck, all in one swift, easy motion. Cody bounced forward, slipped to his knees and came up red-faced and furious.

"I'll get you some day when you haven't got a dozen men to help," he said thickly.

"Don't threaten me, Vic. I can't hold you here, it's true.

53

But I can run you off for trespassing, on the strength of your reputation. Now, beat it!"

Cody scrambled into his truck and slammed the door.

"I might sue you anyway, for assault," he snarled.

"I didn't see you lay a hand on him, Tank," Lefebvre said innocently. "The way I saw it, this man was climbing into his truck and he slipped and fell."

"Bunch of cutthroats, the lot of you. Are you gonna move that heap out of my way?"

"Clay," Rory's father said, "would you move the jeep, please?"

Then Cody gunned his motor furiously and bounced down the road out of sight.

"I hope he breaks an axle and his neck too," Tank Millard said. "Okay, back to work, boys. Rory, I want to talk to you inside. Dutch, you'd better come too."

Inside the toolpush's trailer, his father said, quietly, "Now, Rory, I know that man used to be a scout, one of the worst kind. Maybe still is. But you must be awfully careful about your facts. Now tell us the whole story from the beginning."

Rory repeated everything he'd heard in the restaurant. The men listened carefully. At the end his father said, "Why didn't you tell me all this before?"

"I was afraid you'd say I was just imagining things."

"Hmmf. Well, maybe you are. Anyway, it's very risky accusing a total stranger on that kind of hearsay. You didn't know for sure that Cody was a scout. All you had to go on was a voice in a noisy restaurant."

"Anyway, it doesn't make sense, Rory," said Kruger, who had been deep in thought. "Suppose you did hear them the way you say. If they've already got a man in this camp why would Cody risk coming here? He knew your dad would recognize him."

"He could have been watching camp and have seen dad leave," Rory said. "I heard him tell the other man that as soon as he could, he'd let him know where to leave information. I think maybe that's why he was here."

Tank Millard shook his head doubtfully. "You think that, but you don't know. Dutch, you better keep an eye peeled around the rig. If you see anybody acting funny,

54

you let me know. I'm not worried about the old hands, but we have a lot of new ones this year. I suppose Cody could have got to one of them with money."

"Okay. But I can't understand any decent company hiring him now, if he really is scouting."

"They aren't *all* decent out there, Dutch. You know how much oil is worth these days. Some of those people don't care how they get information as long as they get it."

"Yeah, I suppose you're right," sighed Kruger. "I'll keep an eye open."

Rory started to follow Kruger out the door, but his father called him back. Tank Millard drummed his fingers on the desk top and, as usual, seemed at a loss for words.

"Oh dammit!" he blurted. "I can handle twenty or thirty grown men, but I can't seem to manage you. Rory, I appreciate your taking an interest in the rig. It is important to watch out for scouts, and, as it happens, you spotted a man who might be dangerous. But you did it all wrong." Millard sighed and scratched his head. "If the man is innocent, you could have got us into trouble, accusing him like that. You're lucky I happened along and knew his reputation and could bluff him off. On the other hand, if he is up to something, all you've done is put him on his guard. Now you stick to the kitchen and the books and leave the detective work alone. Okay?"

Rory nodded. He didn't dare speak because he felt like crying and he was too big to cry. It was always the same. His father didn't believe him.

Kruger called from outside, "Rory those two youngsters are here to see you. Sammy and Annie somebody."

Rory brightened and made for the door.

"Rory, I wish you'd tell those kids to stop hanging around."

"But you're going to hire their father for odd jobs."

"Yes, but I'm not hiring *them*. A rig's no place for kids."

"But . . . but, they're my friends."

"Well, they're always underfoot."

Suddenly Rory hated his father: too dumb to know there was a spy right in their midst; didn't like kids just because they were Indians, probably. He turned and

55

looked squarely at Tank Millard and said, "You wouldn't run them off if they were white kids."

Right away he wished he hadn't said it. His father turned red. For a minute Rory thought he was going to strike him.

"I ought to wallop you for talking back to me," his father said thickly. "But I guess I had that coming. Listen, it doesn't matter to me whether they're Indians or not. But I'm trying to run a drill camp here and I don't want it turned into a playground. All right, you can have them here if you like, but I don't want them getting in anybody's way or getting into trouble. That goes for you, too."

Rory nodded again and fled. Outside, Sammy and Annie were waiting patiently in the twilight, staring with interest at the rows of trailers and the towering derrick.

"I'm glad you came over," Rory said. He dug in his pocket. "Want some gum?"

They all had a chew of Spearmint and Rory said gloomily, "I've had an awful day. My father's mad at me. And we had one of the spies here but he got away—a guy named Cody. Boy, he was tough!"

"Awwww! Couldn't you trail him?"

"It wasn't that. The men let him go. They don't think it was him for sure. And I still don't know who the other one is. I don't think it's Cornflakes, after all. I think it's one of our crew all right and that Cody came to talk to him. But there were a lot of men around the rig. It could have been Wirkowski or Clay or Garnett or Reason; they were all there."

"Don't worry," Sammy said cheerfully. "We'll help you find him, hey Annie?"

Annie giggled. "You couldn't even catch a rabbit." She looked at Rory. "He tried to shoot a rabbit three times this morning. Missed."

"Aw, for . . . she thinks she's so smart! Hey, that's what I came to ask you. Can you come hunt some rabbits?"

"It's nearly dark now. Anyway I have to work. I could come tomorrow afternoon."

"We'll be here right after lunch."

"We'd better go now," Annie warned. "Daddy said he'd wallop you if you made us late again."

"If *I* made us late! I don't know why I get all the blame! See you tomorrow, Rory."

Rory quietly went about his work. Lefebvre looked at his downcast face and avoided the usual teasing. All through the meal Rory was silent and tried to stay in the kitchen as much as possible. He had a feeling the crewmen were watching him. Some of them were probably laughing behind his back at his wild stories. Worse than that, one of them—if only he knew which one—was maybe watching for a different reason, probably wondering if Rory knew more than he was telling about that second voice in the Fort Mackenzie restaurant.

Still, no one said a word about that afternoon's events. So, when the table was cleared and the dishes done, Rory peeked into the rec trailer. He didn't feel like going to bed so soon, and the rec trailer was peaceful and pleasant with pipe smoke, the murmur of voices and the flick-flock of playing cards. Rory quietly sat in a corner, hoping no one would notice him.

Just then there was a lull, while Garnett dealt a new hand. Then Wirkowski, who had never spoken directly to Rory before, looked straight at him and said, "Bad business. If you heard what you think you heard in that restaurant, you shouldn't have told the whole camp."

Clay nodded soberly and blinked at Rory from behind his thick spectacles. "That's a fact. If you're right then there's a pretty desperate character in this camp. Not too safe for you, Rory."

Oscar Reason, watching the game but, as usual, not playing, said, "Of course, maybe Rory made a mistake."

Garnett, who was winning tonight and in a good humour, riffled the deck and began skimming cards around the table to each player. "Well now, I think we should stop talking about it. I think maybe Tank ticked him off about all this. And Rory's smart. I'll bet he just forgets the whole thing. Hey Rory?"

Rory shrugged. When they turned back to the game, he slipped out and hurried to bed. He had the feeling that the men were teasing him. Well, maybe one of them wasn't teasing. Was the spy one of those four? If so, had he been giving Rory a warning? But which man was it? He thought about what each man had said, but it merely left him puzzled. Any one of them could have been making an innocent remark—or a threat.

The more he thought about it, the surer he was. Maybe he couldn't prove it to suit his father, but he knew Cody was the oil scout and he knew this was the rig they'd talked about in the restaurant. And he was almost certain that the second man was on this rig. Maybe Cornflakes was mixed up in it, too. But as he curled up in his blankets Rory couldn't get rid of the spooky feeling that somebody in this camp would be watching him from now on. It was a long time before he fell asleep.

9

A Track in the Snow

Sammy and Annie were waiting promptly at one-thirty the next afternoon. It was a jewel of a day, only about ten below zero, sunny and still, the snow fresh and sparkling. Rory carefully toted Lefebvre's .22 rifle, safety catch on, muzzle down, shells in his pocket.

"Where's your rifle, Sammy?"

"My ole granpa was using it all morning, so we have to go back to our place and get it now. It's only five miles."

They trudged down the bush road for a mile, then turned off along the Dogribs' snowmobile trail through the trees.

"We should have snowshoes," Sammy said. "You know how to use them?"

Rory shook his head. "I was never in the bush before this winter. I haven't even hunted much."

"My ole granpa taught me to hunt and track, and my ole man is teaching me about engines," said Sammy. "So I know a lot of stuff that you don't."

"You're lucky," said Rory wistfully. "I wish I were an Indian."

"It's not much fun sometimes," Annie said.

"How come?"

"Oh, it gets awfully cold in the winter. And in the summer there's black flies all the time. And it's not very nice when we go to town."

"Why not?"

"Well, because we're Indians. Once in Yellowknife, some white boys fought Sammy and hurt him. And they chased me."

"They were bigger than me," Sammy said.

"I wouldn't have let them if I'd been there," Rory said fiercely.

Sammy sniffed. "You're not much bigger than I am."

"I don't care. I'd have helped you."

Annie smiled at him. "You're nice. But a lot of white kids tease us."

They walked silently in single file for an hour. Then suddenly they broke into a clearing with a cluster of pre-fabricated houses, each with its snowmobile in front.

"Here's our place." Sammy led the way in. There were two bedrooms and a small living room, sparsely furnished but with a flickering television. In the small kitchen, their mother was cooking stew. Their father, Matthew Football, jumped up and greeted Rory with a grin.

"Your dad said I could come a couple days a week, do a few odd jobs, maybe tune up the jeep. Real good!"

"I'm glad." Rory glanced at grandfather Pierre Football who smiled silently from a corner.

"My ole granpa don't speak much English . . ."

"Doesn't," corrected Annie.

"That's what I *said!* Anyway he never went to school the way my ole man did."

He spoke rapidly to the grandfather in a strange tongue. Pierre Football nodded and Sammy helped himself to a .22 rifle and a pair of snowshoes. Granpa pointed to Rory and spoke again. *"Nezo, nezo!"*

"What's netzo mean?" Rory asked.

"Nezo. It means good. Granpa's glad you're our friend."

Outside again, they plodded through the woods and Sammy picked up a fresh trail. They followed it for a quarter of a mile and suddenly a rabbit sprang up. Sammy fired and missed. Rory didn't even get a shot away.

"Sammy can track good but he can't shoot," snickered Annie.

"Oh yeah, oh yeah? Watch this!"

They took turns shooting at pine cones. Rory, much to his surprise, got one. Sammy hit two. Annie knocked down three.

"Darn ole rifle," Sammy complained. "The ole man ought to get a new one."

"The old one works all right for me," Annie said, and winked behind her brother's back.

"Hunting's not so good today," said Sammy.

"I'd better start back," Rory said. "I have to go to work soon."

"We'll walk back with you." Sammy put on the snowshoes and showed how he could walk through deep snow, looking somewhat like a duck but covering the ground at astonishing speed.

"I wish I could snowshoe," Rory said. "We never do any of that stuff in the city."

"I'll teach you," Sammy said grandly. "Hey, what *do* you do in the city?"

"Well, there's hockey and TV and school and there're thousands of people. And buildings everywhere, higher than the drill rig. And no wild animals. And an awful lot of noise."

Annie shivered. "I don't think I'd like it. I'd be scared."

"I guess you would. There's hundreds and hundreds of cars and you really have to watch out for them."

"I'd like that," Sammy said. "I like engines. Once we were at Fort Rae and the priest there, he had a motorboat that wouldn't work. So me and him took it apart. And he said I had a real . . . real talut or something."

"Talent?"

"Yeah, I guess. That's good, huh?"

"It means you know a lot about engines without being taught."

"That's me all right," said Sammy modestly. "I'm sure good with those engines."

"You're good at a lot of things," Rory said politely. "Like the way you tracked that rabbit a while ago. I couldn't have done that."

"That was nothing. Hey, I wish I could track something really big for you. Look, we're nearly at camp and there's still some daylight. Let me show you how I can really track."

They were just around a bend in the road from the camp; they could hear the drill rig engines. Sammy knelt down in the road. He pointed to a jumble of footprints.

"See, here's where we came along today. There're my tracks, and Annie's; hers are smaller. And there're yours,

61

you've got soles on your boots that leave marks like a tire. And look, here's a man's tracks underneath. He must have been here since midnight last night because it snowed around eleven o'clock. Pretty smart, huh?"

Sammy rose and began padding back along the road in the direction they had just come.

"I can't go back again, Sammy. I have to go to work."

"Just another minute," pleaded Sammy. "See how I can follow this guy's trail. Look, I can tell you about him. He was big: he has a big foot, wears heavy boots. I've lost him. Wait, here he is again. Aw, nuts, he's made it too easy."

For the footprints suddenly veered off the road into deep snow among the trees.

"Let's leave it, I have to get back," Rory said.

"Aw, please, let's follow it a bit more. I can tell you what he was doing, everything."

"I can tell you what he was doing," grumbled Rory. "He was probably going to the bathroom."

"Oh, Rory!" Annie blushed.

But Sammy was already off on the trail, shouting, "Come on." They followed him, wandering in and out among the trees.

"Acts like he was looking for something," Sammy called back. "And he must have been here in the night because, look, he nearly ran into trees a couple of times."

The trail suddenly straightened out and went directly into a small clearing. There, in the middle, a dead poplar stood by itself, bleached grey-white from the weather. The footprints led straight to the tree, then looped away at an angle toward the road.

"Well, there you are, I told you I could follow trail." Sammy leaned against the tree, grinning. Then Annie looked up and gave a little cry. "There's something up there! A letter!"

It *was* a letter, too, or a folded note anyway, wedged in a crack high above their heads.

"Give me a lift," Sammy said. "I think I can reach it." He shinnied up the trunk and Rory boosted him higher. Sammy snatched the note and slid down. They opened it. It was a sheet of ordinary ruled notepaper with a few words printed on it:

SATURDAY, JAN. 16—536 FEET. NEXT REPORT IN THREE OR FOUR DAYS. THIS PLACE IS TOO CLOSE TO CAMP. I WILL LEAVE THE NEXT AT THE OTHER PLACE.

"What's it mean?" said Sammy.

"The spy!" Annie shrieked.

"Of course!" Rory pounded Sammy's arm. "Don't you see? He's telling how deep they've drilled. I was right! There is a spy in our camp. That man Cody got a message to him yesterday. I bet he passed him a note or a map and told him to leave the information here!"

"Let's take it to your father right now," Annie said.

"No, wait." Rory shook his head. "I want to get all the evidence. We've got to find out who the spy is." He frowned and studied the note. "No, I've got it. We'll leave this note right here!"

"You gotta be kidding!" cried Sammy. "The other guy'll come and get it."

"Sure he will. And I'll be hiding right there in the bush to see what he does next. If he goes away, I'll follow him and find his hideout. If he goes to our camp, I'll watch and see who he talks to."

"Oh, Rory, that's clever!" Annie clapped her hands and gave his arm a small squeeze.

"Yeah, not bad," Sammy admitted. "Wish I could come too."

"Why not? We'll do it tonight right after supper."

"Sammy, you know Daddy'll wallop you if you sneak out," Annie warned.

"Yeah, I know. Guess I can't. But look, Rory, you'll get in trouble too if you sneak out."

Rory hesitated. "They'll never miss me. And I'll be right close to camp, so I can get back in a hurry if they call me. And if I get the evidence on Cody, they'll all just have to believe me."

"But what makes you think Cody'll come tonight?"

"Well . . . well, I don't know, but I just have a feeling. See, this note was left last night. I bet Cody arranged it that way. And I bet he'll pick it up as quick as he can, because he has to pass the information on to someone else. But he wouldn't come in the daytime in case someone from the camp saw him. I just hope he doesn't come before I can get here tonight."

They hurried back to the road and Rory raced into camp. He rushed into his chores. Maybe this was the night, the night when he'd settle the mystery of Rory's wildcat.

10

Danger in the Woods

Rory flew through his work at the supper table, swallowed his own dinner, washed the dishes right away and dried them in record time.

"By golly, what's your hurry? You going to the dance tonight?" Lefebvre beamed at his own little joke.

"I've got things to do, René."

"Well, it's okay with me. Seeing's we're finished early, I think I will play a little cards tonight."

Perfect, Rory thought, on his way to his trailer; René won't miss me. Now, what to take along? A flashlight. A chocolate bar: it might be a long wait. Put on plenty of warm clothing, because the kitchen thermometer said eighteen below zero. He pulled on extra socks, a thick sweater, a second pair of trousers, then his parka.

A weapon? Feeling a little foolish, Rory got out the hunting knife his father had given him two Christmases before. It was shiny and clean; he'd never used it, much to his father's disgust. He wasn't at all sure he could use it, if he had to. Still, he felt better with it in his pocket. He glanced at his wristwatch: eight-thirty. He slipped into the night.

It was pitch black, with no moon, and the stars buried under clouds. He picked his way along the bush road. Away from the lights of camp his eyes soon grew used to the dark and he found the turn-off to the lone poplar tree without even using the flashlight. He followed the dark shadows of this afternoon's footprints. Soon he reached the clearing. He stopped at the edge, straining his eyes into the dark. He held his breath and listened. There was only the steady rumble of the drill rig nearby.

He moved to the poplar as silently as the snow would let him. A quick flash of light on the tree. Good, the note was still there.

Now think, Rory told himself. If Cody is going to come,

he'll probably come from the road. Or will he? No, he might come through the bush, rather than risk meeting someone on the road. But which way would he come? Well, surely not from the side closest to the oil rig.

Rory crossed the clearing, toward the sound of the rig. He couldn't see the derrick, because the bush was very thick here, but the comforting mumble of its engines was only about two hundred yards away.

He found a natural nook, well back among the trees and under the low-hanging branches of a spruce. He had an almost clear view of the lone poplar. He curled up and waited.

In a while the sound of the rig became part of the night and then he was able to pick out other noises, as well as sights. Once, quite near, an owl hooted. Then Rory heard the tiny frightened squeak of a small creature. Poor little thing, the owl had got it.

Then came a crack like a pistol shot. Rory's heart skipped a beat. But nothing happened. He remembered reading somewhere that frost will snap tree branches on a very cold night. Certainly this one was cold. He wriggled his fingers and toes to keep the circulation going.

Finally he slipped an arm inside his parka with the flashlight and risked a quick glance at his watch: ten o'clock. A shadow flickered silently across the clearing. Rory held his breath, but it was only a small fox. It sniffed Rory's trail, then fled into the night.

Ten-thirty. He was almost numb with cold. Gingerly, as quietly as possible, he stretched out flat in the snow and flexed his arms and legs. It helped a little but he knew that if he stayed still much longer he would freeze. Another half-hour, then I'll give up, he told himself. Maybe the man wasn't coming tonight. He ate the chocolate bar and curled up again.

Then the footsteps came: no animal this time, at least not a four-footed one. It was a man, crunching steadily in from the direction of the road, making no particular effort to be quiet. Soon he broke into view. Rory could see the outline of snowshoes and a rifle slung against his back. The man paused at the edge of the clearing, then walked straight to the poplar. He stopped again, looked all around and listened. Rory crouched motionless, even holding his breath so that its frozen cloud would not give him away.

A quick beam of light ran up the tree and caught the note. The man plucked it down, cupped a hand around his flashlight and held light and paper close to his face. The soft glow showed the broken nose and the thin cruel line of the mouth. It was Vic Cody all right.

He switched the light off, turned back toward the road, dropped the note, muttered an angry word and snapped the flashlight on again. He fumbled for the note and found it. But then, instead of moving on, he stood studying the snow. He flicked the light to the edge of the clearing and back again, then around the base of the tree. Suddenly the awful truth dawned on Rory: Cody had found their tracks from the afternoon. Now he knew that someone had seen the message. And then, with real horror, Rory realized something else: he had left tracks right to the spot where he was crouching!

It was too late to run now. Cody was back at the tree, playing the flashlight around in the snow. In a moment he picked up Rory's trail. He traced it with the light to the edge of the bush and swept the beam once, quickly, among the trees. The low-hanging spruce bough saved Rory, for the moment.

Cody hesitated. He looked and listened in the direction of the drill rig. Then he reached behind his back, loosened something from his belt and hefted it in his hand. Rory's scalp began to prickle. It was a hatchet!

Slowly, flicking the light on and off, Cody began to move toward him, following the footprints, looking up and listening every few seconds. Rory tried to gather his legs under him but they wouldn't move, too weak from cold, or fright. He thought of screaming, but he knew he would never be heard over the drill rig and then Cody would be on top of him.

His mouth was dry with a funny sort of metal taste in it. His body felt weak and helpless, like in a nightmare when you want to run and can't. He fumbled for the hunting knife, pulled it from the sheath, but he knew it was hopeless. Before I can move he will swing the hatchet,

67

Rory thought. Cody was among the trees now, not twelve feet away.

"Ror-ee!"

It was Lefebvre, somewhere back in the campsite. Vic Cody stopped in his tracks and snapped off the flashlight.

"Halloo there! Rory!" That was Clay. There were other voices now. They had finally missed him. Of course! Lefebvre, good old Lefebvre, had finished his card game and gone back to the trailer. And they'd finally missed him.

Cody hesitated another instant and stared hard into the bush. For one terrible second it seemed that he was looking into Rory's eyes. Then he slipped the hatchet into his belt, turned, and hurried across the clearing toward the path that led to the road. There he paused, hastily changed course, and veered off among the trees at a trot, away from the drill rig. Rory breathed a little prayer of thanks. He had done one thing right, anyway: he had hidden on the side nearest the rig.

He lay under the tree, trembling. The camp was alive with shouts now, but Rory couldn't find the strength to move. Finally he rose on shaky legs, almost toppling over as the blood rushed back into his cramped limbs, and carefully circled the clearing, looking fearfully back over his shoulder. He picked his way out to the road and ran at full tilt into camp.

The place was swarming with men and lights. Kruger was warming up the jeep. His father was organizing search parties. Wirkowski saw him first.

"Here! He's here!"

They crowded round him.

"Where the devil have you been?"

"We thought you were lost."

"Boy, you hadn't oughta wander off at night like that."

Then his father stepped among them and said, "Get over to your trailer, Rory. Thanks for turning out, boys."

Rory stumbled and Lefebvre grabbed him under the arms.

"Come on, I'll give you a hand. Boy, you gave us a scare!"

His father followed them into the trailer. He watched silently as Lefebvre helped Rory strip off his clothes and

68

get under the covers. Rory was shivering so hard that the bed shook, but he couldn't help it. He could see that his father was very angry, but even that was better than what had nearly happened. One more minute, he thought. If Lefebvre hadn't called, he would've had me in one more minute!

"He's got a bad case of the shakes, Boss. I'll get him a hot drink."

"Thanks, René." Now he was alone with his father. Finally Tank Millard said quietly, "I'm not going to ask where you were or what you were doing, Rory. It doesn't matter. It was just about the stupidest thing on earth. Nobody goes wandering in the bush at night in this country. You turned this whole camp on its ear. You kept men up when they should have been getting their rest. You scared us half to death."

His father got up and walked to the door.

"Now this is the last time, absolutely. One more crazy stunt and I ship you back to Edmonton and into a boarding-house. Understand?"

Rory nodded. His teeth were chattering too much for him to speak.

"All right. Get some sleep." His father was gone and Lefebvre was back with a mug of scalding hot chocolate. Rory sipped it, and gradually the shivering stopped. Lefebvre threw another blanket over him and turned out the light. In a while Rory slept, but it was a restless sleep. Once he dreamed that Cody was standing over him, laughing, the hatchet raised ready to strike, and Rory came awake screaming in the middle of the night.

11

Theft in the Night

To Rory's surprise, hardly anyone mentioned the incident the next morning. Lefebvre teased, "That must have been quite a dance you went to," but when Rory didn't answer, he dropped the subject. Everyone else seemed to assume that it was just another of those crazy things you could expect from the boss's kid, and left it at that. In a way it was humiliating, but in another way it was lucky.

Sammy and Annie dropped in a few afternoons later and Rory told his story.

"This is getting good!" cried Sammy. "When do we go after Cody again?"

"We don't," Rory said. "Or, anyway, I don't."

"You scared?"

"Oh, Sammy, leave Rory alone!"

"Sure, I'm scared," Rory said soberly. "He just about killed me with a hatchet!"

"I wish you'd tell your father what happened," Annie said, with a worried frown.

"That'd just get me into more trouble. I didn't find out who the spy is. All I did was disobey my father. He's mad now, and if he found out why I was out the other night, he'd ship me back to Edmonton for sure."

"So what do we do? Just let the spy go ahead and spy?"

"Sammy, I'm just going to stay out of trouble for a while. If we see anybody stealing information, sure we can tell my father. But it'll have to be real proof. He's pretty hard to convince."

Days and weeks went by. Rory's wildcat bored steadily into the earth. If information was still being passed to Cody, Rory could see no evidence of it. He watched the men closely, listened to their talk, but learned nothing. Often crewmen wandered away from camp, alone or in twos, to hunt or prowl in their spare time. One of them might be meeting Cody somewhere. But the memory of that night beside the poplar clearing was enough to discourage Rory from following them.

His lessons were coming along well. Harvey Clay dropped in two or three times a week to help him. Clay was pretty smart, but Rory didn't really like him. He was too smart. He was forever talking about making fast money.

Still, maybe you couldn't blame him for being that way. One afternoon when they'd finished a lesson on farmers, Clay closed the book and said bitterly, "My old man took me out of school, soon as I was old enough, and put me to work on the farm. I stuck it for four years, then got out. I finally finished high school, a couple of years ago. Then I took a year at university until I ran out of money."

"Didn't you like farming?"

"It wasn't a matter of liking it. My old man didn't know how to farm: no decent machinery, no decent livestock. He couldn't even keep books. He could hardly write his name. He didn't know anything and he didn't have anything."

Rory felt uncomfortable. He tried to think of something to say, but Clay didn't seem to need a reply. He flipped through a textbook without looking at it, then banged it shut.

"Our family was the laughing-stock of the neighbourhood. They called us hillbillies!" He got up and walked about the room. "I said to myself when I got out of there, 'Nobody's ever going to laugh at me again.' People are going to respect me, Rory. Nobody respects you if you don't know anything. Or if you don't have money. Money, that's what you need first. By next fall, I'll have enough to get out of this business, I guarantee it."

"What's wrong with this business?" said Lefebvre suddenly from the bottom bunk, where he'd been napping after lunch. "Lots of good men in this business."

"I'm sick and tired of pitching hay and wrestling drill pipe," Clay said. "I'm getting my law degree and then I'm getting into politics. The lawyers know all the angles. And in politics, boy, you can lay your hands on all sorts of juicy deals." Clay pulled on his parka. "Keep at the books, kid. And come and see me in a few years. I'll fix you up with a nice soft job in government." He winked and slammed the door. Rory stayed at his desk. There was something wrong inside Clay. He made everything seem kind of dirty and sneaky.

Then Lefebvre said quietly, "Don't pay too much attention to Harvey. He is a young man in too much of a hurry. Somebody will tread hard on his toes one of these days."

Rory nodded absently. He was thinking: It certainly wouldn't be hard to imagine Clay spying on his own drill rig for ten thousand dollars.

"Comment ça va?" Lefebvre grinned, seeing his worried frown. And Rory had to grin back and say, "Pretty good. I mean, *Très bien, merci."* Lefebvre was teaching him some French, and some day, he promised, they would go to Montreal and to the restaurant *Les Filles du Roy* and Rory would speak to the waitress in French and order onion soup and snails. Ah yes, Lefebvre was his very good friend. That was one of the happy things about being here.

But the best days were Saturdays and Sundays. Those were the Rory-and-Sammy-and-Annie days. Sometimes Lefebvre would say, "Take the noon hour off," and give them a package of sandwiches and cookies. And they would prowl the bush all day.

Rory's legs were hard with muscle now and no longer trembled when he walked a few miles. His city pallor was gone and he had gained five pounds. He learned to snowshoe on Sammy Football's battered shoes. Then one day Lefebvre called them all into the kitchen. "Surprise!" he cried and held up three new pairs of medium-size snowshoes he'd had sent in from Edmonton. For once Sammy was speechless. Rory forgot that he was nearly grown up and gave the cook a bear hug. Annie ran and kissed him on the chin.

"Hey!" Lefebvre beamed. "You are nice kids. Maybe I take you all home with me."

"Yeah, sure, René, all you need is three more children," teased Rory, and Lefebvre laughed until the tears came.

After that they roamed farther than ever. They carefully

avoided old Cornflakes's cabin but they went in all other directions. They found two or three other cabins, all seemingly deserted by trappers of years gone by.

Gradually, Rory learned that the North was not nearly as bleak and empty as it had seemed that first day on the Mackenzie Highway. It would, of course, freeze you to death if you were stupid enough to stay unsheltered too long. It would get you lost if you failed to read its signs. But it also had peace and calm that washed your mind clear of gloomy thoughts. And if, instead of fighting the North, you let it teach you, there were many things to learn. There were families of ptarmigan and juncos and fox at play for the silent watcher; here the dainty footprints of a caribou; there a tale of tragedy in the snow: a rabbit's path, then a wolf's footprints picking up the trail, the one following the other for a half-mile, a frantic chase, the signs of a tussle, blood, bits of fur, then one set of prints—the wolf's—leaving the scene.

Sammy and Annie were learning about Rory's world, too. One day Sammy said, "Hey, you know something? I've never seen how that old rig of yours works."

"How it works? Well, there it is. Take a look."

"No, I mean what're they really doing? Can't we go up close and watch?"

"Well, all right, but don't get in the way. They're coring now."

"What's that?"

"I'll show you," Rory said importantly.

The crew had just pulled up the core bit—the hollow cutting tool that looked something like a doughnut with tiny chips of stone round its rim. They shook a smooth cylinder of rock from inside it. The rock was wet and dirty-looking but everybody seemed pleased, especially Rory's father who was overseeing the job. He even smiled at Rory and gave him a little pat on the shoulder. "Came to have a look, eh? Well, you've been real good kids lately. Stick around." He picked up a piece of core. "Look. That rock came from a mile down. How about that?"

"Is that really rock?" Sammy said suspiciously. "You can't cut rock as smooth as that."

Tank Millard pointed to the core bit. "See those chips around the edge? They're diamonds."

"Diamonds!"

"Not the kind you have in rings. They're called industrial diamonds. They're very hard and good for cutting. When you get the weight of all those tons of drill stem—the pipe, I mean—pushing down, well, this thing cuts rocks as smooth as butter."

He bent over the cores again with Oscar Reason. On the derrick floor the day crew, in overalls and safety helmets, were getting ready for regular drilling again. Clay and a squat farm boy named Jensen lifted the regular drill bit—a heavy thing with three wheels, each with sharp cutting teeth—and screwed it to a length of pipe hanging down from the derrick.

The driller, Wirkowski, worked the controls. The engines hummed. The bit and length of pipe disappeared down the drill hole, until only its top end showed. The crew locked it firmly in place. High above in the derrick, Garnett was guiding down another piece of pipe, dangling from a block and tackle. As it came down near them, Clay and Jensen seized it with enormous tongs, fitted its threaded end into the threaded end of the piece of pipe sticking up from the hole. They threw a few hitches of chain round it. The engines growled again. The chain spun the two pieces of pipe tightly together. Then the new length went down the hole.

Crash, clang, whirr, spin, rumble. Screw the pipe together, send it down the hole, get another pipe, all in sixty seconds. They did it again and again, as smoothly as an army drill team, as sure-footed as dancers in spite of their big boots. In less than an hour they were finished. The bit was at the bottom, ready to chew its way farther into the earth. Wirkowski, silent as always, watched his controls. The song of the engines changed pitch; they were working hard again. The crew relaxed. Rory and the Footballs turned away.

"All right!" Sammy let out a long breath. "That's neat. I think I'll do that, instead of being a hockey player."

Oscar Reason, gathering up his core samples, overheard. He stopped and grinned. This must really be a good day, Rory thought; even Oscar's smiling.

"You kids interested in all this?"

"You better believe it!"

"Want to see the cores?"

"You bet!"

"Come over to the trailer."

Oscar's trailer reminded Rory of a museum. There were rock samples everywhere, and a microscope, and bottles of acid. There were strange-looking maps, some with rows and rows of wavy lines, some that showed different layers of the earth and some that looked like maps of North America only they couldn't be, because the land and oceans were in the wrong places.

Reason stripped off his parka and set the box of cores on his work table. He said, "You kids know where oil comes from?"

"Sure," Sammy said. "There's a big lake of it down under there someplace."

"That's what a lot of people think. It's not like that. Take off your coats a while." Reason lit his pipe. "This is a kind of mystery story. I hear you like mysteries, Rory."

Rory said nothing. Was Reason making fun of him?

"A long, long time ago, millions of years ago, this part of the world was an ocean," the geologist went on. Sammy said, "Aw, come on, Mr. Reason."

"No, I'm serious. Right where we are now was all ocean. The world hasn't always been the way it is now, you see." He pointed to the funny maps of North America. "Well, there were fish and all sorts of other water creatures in that ocean. They died, the way everything does sooner or later, and their bodies fell to the bottom. This went on year after year, for thousands of years." Reason puffed on his pipe and looked at the maps. "Millions of years went by. The seas went away for a while, and came back, and went away again. The bodies of those little creatures were covered with sand and clay, sometimes thousands of feet thick."

"What's this have to do with oil?" Rory said.

"I'm coming to that. Well, the layers built up and the pressure built up, too, and that sand and clay turned

76

to sandstone and shale, what we call sedimentary rock. The bones and shells of those little creatures turned to stone—you must have heard about fossils in school, Rory? And from their bodies came little drops of oil."

"What turned them to oil?" Annie asked.

"We don't know all the reasons. Partly the pressure. Partly the heat. It's hot way down there, you know. And other things we're not sure of."

"So they all turned into a lake down there?"

"No, Sammy, they're all tiny drops in the pores of the rock. The rock's something like a sponge. See, on this core? See the spaces in the rock? That's where we find oil."

Rory lifted the heavy core. "So this is where you look for clues?"

"That's right. I'll test this, and then I'll send it to the head office laboratory and they'll test it more. This is a pretty important piece of rock, you see."

"My father said that if a piece of core had signs of oil in it and the opposition got hold of it, it might be worth thousands of dollars to them."

Reason looked up at Rory in surprise. "That's true. If the other companies could be sure they'd find oil, the information would be worth an awful lot of money. You see, oil's getting awfully scarce, Rory, and awfully expensive. So they'd bid high for the nearby land." Reason hefted the rock core thoughtfully. "Yes, the information in a little piece of rock like this could even be worth millions."

"Wow!" Sammy said. "Millions of dollars! I can't even figure what millions would look like!"

"Neither can I," said Reason. "I'm just as broke as you are. But what I'm saying is absolutely true. Listen, it's costing WestCan close to a million bucks just to drill this well. If it's a dry hole, that's money down the drain. But if we hit oil or gas, and find more wells around, it'll *really* be worth millions. Yep, I could get a lot of money for one of these dirty pieces of rock, if I wanted to." He laughed and put the core aside, but he didn't sound as if he were really joking. "Well, I'd better get to work," he said finally.

After they were outside, Sammy said, "Did you hear what he said about needing money?"

Rory nodded. "He'd be in a good spot to pass information to Cody, too. I ought to keep a closer watch on him."

It was beginning to snow, and Sammy and Annie hurried home. That night Rory dreamed that an icy ocean was flowing down from the Arctic. It surrounded the drill rig, rose higher and higher in the trailer, washed over his bed. Then he woke up and found he'd kicked the blankets off. The trailer was getting cool, and it was half-past six. He flung on his clothes, dashed to the wash-trailer and on to the kitchen.

"Sorry, René. I slept in."

"That's okay. I'm sorry you have to work on Sunday, but then we all do here. Okay, seven o'clock, the men'll be coming."

But the men did not come hurrying in as usual. Ten past seven. Quarter past.

"What is keeping those guys?" Lefebvre demanded. "The eggs are getting cold." He looked out the window. "Hey something's going on! Look at the crowd over by Oscar's trailer. Run over and see what's the matter, will you?"

Rory scurried across the campsite. Oscar Reason was talking in a loud, angry voice to Rory's father, who listened with a grim expression. All the day crew and night crew were there, their faces serious too. Rory tugged at Clay's sleeve and whispered, "What's wrong?"

"Somebody got into Reason's trailer overnight. Stole all of yesterday's core samples."

12

The Spy

"All right," Tank Millard was saying. "Simmer down, Oscar, and let's sort this out. When was the last time you saw the cores?"

"I finished up about ten-thirty last night. Then I boxed them up for shipping to the lab."

"Were you out of the trailer after that?"

"I was over to the kitchen for coffee, from about quarter after eleven until midnight."

"Did you lock the trailer while you were away?"

"Well . . . well, no. I never do. There's nobody around but our crew. What would they want with my stuff?"

"That's what I aim to find out," Millard said grimly. "On the other hand, maybe it was somebody else—like my old friend Cody."

"Good Lord, Tank, surely he wouldn't have the nerve to walk right into this camp, even in the dark."

"The only thing Cody has is nerve. Well, were the cores there when you got back from coffee last night? And if they weren't, how come you're just finding out now?"

Reason looked sheepish. "Well, whoever took them played me for a sucker. There was a core box there when I got back, right where I left it. Only it was an empty one, I found out this morning. They all look alike, you know, Tank. The only difference between them is in the markings I paint on the outside to show the depth of the particular samples. And I make up several of these in advance."

"And when you came in last night you didn't check the box to see if it was the one with yesterday's sample?"

"Well, why should I? The place was in order. It looked exactly the way I left it. And I was dead tired. So I went right to bed. I didn't find out they'd been switched until just now."

Millard nodded. "Well, I guess I don't have to tell you

s serious. We may have lost valuable informa-
~~d,~~ in any case, this is theft. We'll have to get to the
~~o~~ttom of it. I'm going to get the Mountie from Mackenzie
to search every inch of this camp, starting with my own
trailer."

He turned away, then added, "I'm going to call him
right now. Day-shift men, get breakfast and carry on as
usual. I'd appreciate it if the rest of you didn't wander out
of camp today until the Mountie's finished. And Oscar,
from now on, padlock that door!"

Rory walked slowly back to the kitchen trailer. The men
followed in hushed little groups. They ate quietly, talking
in low voices about the theft, sometimes glancing uncom-
fortably at each other. Was this the work of an insider?
Now they all remembered Rory's story of the restaurant
plot. Maybe the kid wasn't so crazy after all. Maybe somebody at this very table was a spy. They filed out silently
and went to their trailers to sleep or read.

Rory dried the breakfast dishes and went outside. He
looked in vain for Annie and Sammy. He moped around
the rig, then went back to his trailer. Lefebvre was writing
a letter. Rory pulled out his math book but he couldn't
concentrate on the problems. His mind kept drifting back
to the bigger problem: who was the spy?

"René," he said finally, "who played cards last night?"

"Hmmm? Oh, same ones as usual: Wirkowski, Clay,
Garnett. I think. Yes, Garnett was there. And Jensen and
Dutch."

"What about Oscar?"

"Oscar? Oh, he came in, got a coffee about eleven-
fifteen, sat around and watched them a while. He didn't
play himself."

"Did anybody quit the game while Oscar was there?"

"Quit the game? N-o-o, nobody quit. Those boys are
all on day shift, you see. They played until a little after
midnight, five or ten minutes after Oscar left."

"And they stayed right there the whole time Oscar was
there?"

"How'm I ever going to get this letter off? . . . Sure, I
think they stayed. Wait a minute. No, Garnett went out for

a few minutes—you know, to the toilet or something. Hey, are you playing detective again? Your dad will blow his top if you start that again, Rory."

"I was just wondering."

"You were just wondering, eh? Maybe wondering if old Garnett stole the cores? Well, he'd have to have rockets on his feet to get over there, steal them, take them out of camp, hide them and get back as quick as he did. And he certainly wouldn't hide 'em inside camp, where everybody would start looking for them! No, I don't think you are a very good detective, Rory." Lefebvre chuckled and went back to his letter.

In mid-morning a Royal Canadian Mounted Police constable drove in with Rory's father. A little flurry of excitement ran through the camp.

"Sure didn't take the Mountie long to get going," Lefebvre said.

"Tank phoned him this morning," said Dutch Kruger. "The Mountie came up the highway by car as far as our road. Tank met him there. The Mountie's car never would have made it over our road."

The constable was a tall, serious young man in a dark blue parka and a fur hat. He went quickly to work. He searched each trailer and talked briefly to every man. He spent a long time in Oscar Reason's trailer. Then he went outside and carefully prowled around the campsite. He had been in camp nearly four hours when he paused behind the kitchen trailer, studied the snow and called Oscar Reason. Reason looked at the ground, ran back to his trailer and returned with a core box.

Rory's father and Dutch Kruger joined them, and Rory drew near to listen.

"Find something?" Tank Millard asked.

"Not much," the Mountie said. "Looks as though our man set the box down here, maybe to rest a minute. See this imprint in the snow? It's the same size as the box Mr Reason has here."

"That makes sense," said Rory's father. "Those boxes weigh more than a hundred pounds when they're full. A man would want to rest now and then."

"And there's no other boxes in camp shaped quite the same," said Reason. "It was a core box all right."

"So now what?" Rory's father asked.

"Not much, I'm afraid." The constable glanced around the campsite. "This place is a mess of footprints. There's no way of knowing where the man went from here. About all I can say is that he probably went away from the camp. I've searched everywhere and there are no cores. As for the men, several of them were by themselves between eleven and twelve, but I have no reason to suspect any of them. There just isn't enough evidence, Mr Millard."

"Well, thanks for coming. I'll drive you back to your car."

"Thanks. I'm sorry I can't stay overnight and look around some more tomorrow. I'd like to hunt up that old trapper and have a talk, and the Dogribs, too. And that fellow Cody."

"Can't be helped," Millard said. "You say you have to fly south to a murder trial in the morning?"

"Yes. Can't postpone it. And I don't know how long I'll be away. But I promise you I'll look into all this as soon as I get back."

They drove away. The men drifted back to their trailers. Rory stood by the kitchen, looking at the mark in the snow. There was something wrong about this, some important fact that escaped him at the moment. Vic Cody was mixed up in it, surely. But no matter what his father said, Rory couldn't believe that Cody would walk right into camp, steal the box, stop for a rest right outside the trailer where men were playing cards, then boldly walk on. He remembered how Cody had fled from the sound of the voices that night in the clearing. He acted like a man who didn't take unnecessary risks.

No, there was a missing clue in this mystery. If only he could sort it out.

"Hey, Rory."

Sammy Football was calling softly from the trees at the edge of camp. Annie was beside him. Behind them, grinning broadly, stood Pierre Football. Rory hurried over.

"Where have you been? I was waiting."

"Ole granpa said he'd take us hunting and we came to

get you too, after lunch. But granpa saw the Mountie, so we hid back here."

"Ever since lunch?"

"Uh-huh."

"But why?"

"My granpa is kind of scared of Mounties."

"But the Mountie wasn't looking for him."

"He says Mounties are always putting Indians in jail for something."

"Sammy, does your grandfather know anything about these rock cores?"

"What rock cores?"

"Well, I guess that answers my question. Somebody stole Oscar's rock samples last night."

"Yeah? The ones we were looking at?"

"Yes. And they think it was Cody. Only I'm not so sure."

"Maybe granpa could help," Annie said. "He's awfully good at following tracks."

Tracks: maybe that was the answer! There was no hope of finding a trail in camp; it was full of footprints. But if someone had carried the box away, then his tracks ought to show up outside camp. There had been a fresh fall of snow the night before, in the early evening, and nobody had left camp since, except Rory's father.

"If someone left here with a box last night, could your grandfather find the tracks now?"

"Maybe." Sammy turned to the old man, who had been trying, without much luck, to follow the conversation. He spoke rapidly in Dogrib. Pierre Football replied sharply, shaking his head.

"He says he doesn't want any trouble with the police."

"He won't get into trouble. The Mountie's gone and my father won't be back for an hour. Look, we've time before dark. Please?"

Sammy spoke in Dogrib again. Pierre Football nodded. He spoke to Sammy and made a circle in the snow with his foot.

"He says okay," Sammy reported. "He says we should go right around camp and see if tracks come out somewhere."

They moved off with Pierre in the lead. They circled the camp once but, except for the Footballs' own trail and a few rabbit tracks, there was nothing.

"What a bummer!" Rory said. "He must have gone down the road."

"Anybody else been on the road today?" Sammy asked.

"Not that I know of. They were all supposed to stay in camp."

"Maybe granpa can find something."

They moved on to the road. Pierre Football, still in the lead, criss-crossed back and forth, studying the ground. Rory's father had already driven the trail three times that day and the tire treads seemed to be the only marks in sight. Then Pierre Football raised a hand, stopped and knelt down. He called sharply in Dogrib, and pointed to footprints, almost wiped out by the jeep.

They followed the prints for half a mile. Suddenly Annie cried, "Oh, it's snowing again!" And it was: the fat flakes were fluttering down lazily from the darkening sky. Rory's heart sank. It seemed as though everything was against them.

But Pierre Football cried out again. They had reached a right-angle bend in the road, the only one for miles, and here the man's trail turned off abruptly. It was clear and easy to follow now. It moved a few yards into the bush and stopped beside a large triangular rock. There behind the rock was the unmistakable print of a core box. Then the prints turned back to the road. A second track led to the rock from back in the bush. It, too, paused at the rendezvous point, then returned in the direction it had come. The whole story lay before them in the snow.

Pierre Football waved the children back and carefully studied the trails. Then he spoke in Dogrib.

"My Granpa sure knows his stuff," Sammy said proudly. "He says the man from your camp was carrying something heavy: must have been the box. He left it for the guy in the woods. The guy from the woods was about ordinary size. The guy from your camp was pretty big."

"Aw, come on, Sammy, let's stop kidding around! He can't know all that from footprints."

84

"Yes, he does, Rory," Annie said. She spoke to her grandfather. He grinned and rattled off an answer.

"Here's how he knows," Annie explained. "The man from camp had deeper footprints when he came than when he left. And he took shorter steps on the way in too. With the man from the bush it was the other way around. That's how granpa knows the one man carried something in, the second man carried it away."

"What about their size?"

"Well, look, here's the footprints of the man from your camp, bigger than granpa's, and deeper, too, even without his load. But the other man was not so big."

"Cody?" cried Rory.

"Maybe."

The air was full of snow now, like white candy floss. The tracks leading into the bush were filling up fast. Pierre Football looked at them and at the gathering darkness and shook his head.

"No use," Sammy said glumly. "We'll have to quit. We'll walk back with you. What a drag! We were so close to finding out."

"Yes, and there's no telling where he went," Rory said. "He could have circled back to the road and driven away, or gone to one of those empty cabins we saw, or gone to another drill rig."

They walked toward the distant rumble of the WestCan rig. Soon the derrick lights were in sight. Rory's mind went over the clues for the hundredth time. Somebody had walked this road last night, between eleven-fifteen and midnight. It could not have been a man from the night shift because they had all been on duty.

It couldn't have been Oscar Reason himself, not if Pierre Football's trail-reading was correct. Oscar was small, and the spy was a big man. So it had to be somebody from the day shift. But they were playing cards all the time that Reason was out of his trailer. Nobody had left the game—except Garnett for a few minutes, and that sure wasn't enough time to come away out here.... Rory stopped in his tracks.

"I've got it! I know! I know the spy! It's Jim Garnett!"

13

Kidnapped

Pierre Football grinned inquiringly. Annie and Sammy looked puzzled.

"Why Jim Garnett? How can you be so sure, Rory?"

"Look, I know, well, I'm pretty sure, that it has to be one of the day shift, or else somebody like Oscar or René. It wasn't either of them, if your granpa is right about the size of the man: they're both small. Well, there's only three big men on the day shift: Wirkowski, Clay and Garnett."

"Well?"

"Well, the only time they could have stolen the box was last night between quarter after eleven and twelve o'clock, when Oscar was having coffee. They were all playing cards then, but Garnett left for a few minutes."

"But, Rory, he couldn't steal the box and come all the way down here and be back in four or five minutes."

"He didn't come all the way down here right then. He left the box behind the kitchen trailer and went back to the game. The Mountie found box marks there today."

"I get it!" Sammy said. "Then, after the game, Garnett sneaked out of camp when nobody was looking and left the box for Cody."

"That's how it looks. Garnett shares a trailer with a couple of night-shift men. They'd be at work and nobody would know how late he was out."

"Oh, Rory, you really are smart!" Annie gave an excited little hop.

"Yeah, that sounds pretty darn good," Sammy admitted. He translated the conversation for his grandfather. Pierre Football listened closely. Then he grinned at Rory. *"Nezo!* Pretty-darn-good!"

"You'd better get back, Rory, or they'll be mad at you again," warned Annie.

"Gee, you're right. Dad'll be back any minute. Well, maybe I'll see you during the week. And I'll keep an eye on Garnett. All we need now is to catch him in the act. But I won't tell my father until we do."

"You be careful," Sammy said. The Football family vanished into the snowstorm.

That night at supper Rory tried hard not to stare at Garnett but he couldn't help it. Once Garnett looked up and caught his eye. He raised his eyebrows, then frowned, and Rory hurried to fetch more milk.

He watched Garnett as much as possible the next day, and the next, and all that week. Nothing happened except that on Friday Garnett stopped him outside the kitchen after dinner and said, "Something the matter? Seems like everywhere I go I see you hanging around giving me the eye."

Rory forced a grin.

"No, there's nothing wrong."

"You worried about something?"

"Uh . . . no."

"Hey, if you're worried about that fuss over the rock core the other day, forget it. You know what I think? I think Oscar got them mixed up and he's ashamed to admit it. A guy who stays by himself as much as he does, he goes a little funny in the head. Know what I mean?" And Garnett tapped his forehead significantly.

"I don't think he's funny in the head," Rory said.

"Yeah? Well, anyway, stop hanging around me all the time. You make me nervous." There was a tiny edge of warning in his voice.

So, through the next week, Rory was more cautious. He watched Garnett now from windows: from the kitchen, the washroom, his own trailer. Not once, as far as he knew, did the big man do anything unusual. What happened at night was maybe another story, but Rory didn't care to find out.

Another Friday came. The rig had been drilling for nearly ten weeks. It had moved through one sedimentary rock formation into a deeper one. The evening shift had just taken over. Rory went outdoors to stretch his legs, his brain soggy with mathematics. There was still an hour and a half until supper chores. The daylight was lasting longer now. It would soon be spring. He wished Sammy and Annie would drop in.

Then it came: a wild shout from the rig. Kruger ran to the office trailer. Rory heard him cry, "Oil! There's a show of oil in the mud." Tank Millard ran to the rig.

The men from the day shift came hurrying back. Wirkowski with fresh shaving-soap still on his chin, Garnett with his parka swinging open, Clay with his parka hastily draped over his undershirt. Lefebvre stuck his head out the door as Rory joined the race. "What is it?"

"They've struck oil, I guess! But I don't see it gushing. I thought it always gushed up."

"No, no, not any more. They bring it in nice and easy. Wait for me!" Lefebvre ran out in his apron.

Rory wriggled into the crowd and heard Oscar Reason say, "No doubt about it, Tank. We're not right into it yet but we soon will be."

"Yay!" someone bellowed. "Tomorrow Millard buys cigars for the camp."

Millard grinned happily. "That's a deal!" he promised. He looked at Rory and smiled. "There you are, son. Your wildcat struck oil."

Somehow Rory couldn't get excited. There was something unfinished about it all. That old strange feeling of trouble-yet-to-come was suddenly back with him again. Surely the spy wouldn't . . . The spy! He looked around for Garnett: not in the crowd. Rory squeezed out and looked again. The door to the office trailer was quietly closing on someone—and it wasn't his father or Dutch.

Rory moved stealthily to the door and paused. Yes, that was Garnett's voice inside. What was the man doing? Softly, Rory turned the handle and eased the door open a crack.

"V FOR VICTOR," Garnett was saying urgently. "V FOR VICTOR. DO YOU READ ME? COME IN, V FOR VICTOR." Then there was silence, broken only by crackling sounds. Suddenly Rory understood. Garnett was on the two-way radio, trying to send a message: to Vic Cody, probably. Rory hesitated. The others were still milling round the rig. Should he call his father now? No, wait a moment longer;

let Garnett say something that would betray him for sure. Get the facts, like his father said.

"V FOR VICTOR, V FOR VICTOR, COME IN, COME IN." There was no reply, only more static. "Rotten radio," Garnett snarled, and rose with a noisy clump of boots. Rory let go of the door knob and scooted for the corner of the trailer. But Garnett, already at the door, heard the click of the latch. With a bound he was out and round the corner before Rory had gone a half-dozen steps. Rory started to scream, but a big hand smothered his mouth. Only then did he realize his error: he should have run straight for the rig, not round here. Now they were out of sight of the camp.

"You little sneak!" Garnett hissed. "I might have known you were on to something, the way you've been hanging around."

Rory kicked and struggled, but Garnett held him easily. With one hand still pinching his mouth shut, he picked Rory up and dived into the trees behind the office. Out of sight of the rig he stopped, set Rory on his feet, still holding his mouth, and looked back over his shoulder. Then he said, "Well, kid, neither one of us can go back now." He whipped a woollen scarf from his neck, wrapped it tightly round Rory's mouth and tied it with a jerk. Then he took a handful of Rory's collar and shoved. "March. We've got a long way to go."

Rory dragged his feet but Garnett lifted him and shook him until his teeth rattled. They moved on a few steps. Suddenly Rory broke loose and darted aside. Garnett had him again in two long strides and slapped him twice, full in the face. Through the humming in his ears he heard Garnett say angrily, "Now you behave and you won't get hurt. I don't want to rough you up but I sure will if you pull one more stunt like that."

Rory walked along peaceably then, biding his time, going as slowly as he dared. If he could only kill time, surely they would miss him back at camp. But as time went by and it grew dark he began to lose hope. Where was Garnett taking him? Rory had lost his bearings, but the man seemed to know exactly where he was going.

In half an hour Garnett stopped. "Must be hard breath

ing with that thing on your mouth. I guess I can take it off. Don't try to shout. Nobody'll hear you and you'll just make me mad. Understand?"

Rory nodded. Garnett untied the scarf. Rory took a deep breath of frosty air and felt his jaw. It was sore, but nothing else was wrong. Garnett squatted to rest and eyed him curiously.

"How'd you figure out it was me?"

Rory said nothing.

"Won't tell, eh? Doesn't matter. Only I'm sorry you did. I kind of like you and I hate to have to drag you around like this. If you'd just kept your nose out of it, I'd have gone my way and nothing would have happened. WestCan would just have been out of a little information, that's all."

Rory looked at the snow.

"You won't get away with it. My dad'll find you and they'll put you in jail."

"No, they won't. By tomorrow, I'll have my money and me on my way out of the country."

"You can't take me with you. That'd be kidnapping."

"Jeez, Rory, I never planned to take you with me." Garnett sighed and heaved himself to his feet. "I don't now what's going to happen to you. I'll just leave that p to Vic Cody."

14

In the Hands of a Killer

There was no use pretending to be brave. Rory was scared. He'd known all along that Vic Cody was mixed up in the mystery, but somehow he'd never dreamed that he would end up in Cody's hands. He thought of that harsh voice in the restaurant, so many weeks ago, saying, "I don't care how I get information, but I get it." He remembered the murderous look on the man's face that night in the clearing. He thought about the upraised hatchet. Suddenly Rory felt a little sick.

He was tired and hungry, too, which didn't help. It was slow, hard walking in the dark. An hour passed. It began to snow. Garnett still seemed to know where he was going. Another half-hour. They stopped for breath.

"It's less than a mile now," said Garnett. He looked at Rory admiringly. "You've got a lot of guts for a kid. Too bad you're such a snoop. You could be home safe and warm right now."

Finally they came to a clearing, with a small cabin at the foot of a hill. There was something familiar about the place.

"Why, that's old Cornflakes's cabin!" cried Rory.

"Who?"

"The old trapper that fought Wirkowski back in Mackenzie."

"Yeah? Well, I've been there lots of times lately and there's no old trapper here now. Come on."

They trudged wearily the last few yards. The snow had turned into a blizzard. Garnett hammered on the door. Immediately a light went out inside. Garnett knocked again.

"Open up. It's me, Garnett."

The door opened a crack. Cody's voice barked from the darkness inside. "Who's that with you?"

"The Millard kid. Nobody else."

Cody swung the door open. "Hurry up. Get in."

He relit the coal-oil lamp.

"Now what the devil is this all about? What's the idea of coming over here with that kid?"

"Relax," Garnett said wearily. "I'll tell you everything. You got some coffee? And any grub?"

"There's stew in the pot. Come on, hurry up, what's the kid doing here? What're you doing here?"

Garnett flung off his parka and stood over the little woodstove. Its sides glowed red. A coffee pot and a stew pot bubbled on top. Suddenly Rory felt so shaky from hunger and fatigue that he simply slid to the floor, parka still on, and leaned against the wall.

"They got a show of oil this afternoon," Garnett said, warming his hands. "I tried to radio. I couldn't get you."

"I've had the radio on all afternoon."

"I bet you haven't been getting anything."

"No, that's right. If that stinking radio is broken down now, right when I need it..." Cody swore. Then he looked at Rory. "What about him?"

"He caught me on the radio. I grabbed him and took off into the bush. I had to bring him along or he'd have spilled everything."

"I can think of a couple other things you could have done with him," Cody said savagely. He walked over, took Rory by the collar, and pulled him to his knees. "The dirty little spy! He's been nothing but trouble right from the start. I ought to break his neck."

"Aw, leave him alone," Garnett said. "He can't do us any harm now. Nobody believed anything he said back there. By the time Millard and that dumb Dutchman Kruger catch on to us, you and I'll be gone."

"It won't be easy now," Cody snapped. "The whole countryside will be after us in the morning, just because of this rotten kid, and because you were stupid enough to let him catch you."

"Can't we radio your people tonight? Get them to fly us out first thing in the morning?"

"We'll have to. We've got the news they want, so we can collect our money. They'll get us to Edmonton. Then

94

you go your way and I'll go mine and if I never see you again it'll be too soon!"

He turned to the two-way radio. "I wonder if this thing will work now."

"I'm going to have some grub," Garnett said. "Okay if I feed the kid?"

"Feed him? I'll feed him to the foxes! Ah, do what you like, I'll settle with him later." Cody sat down before the radio and twiddled the dials.

Garnett spooned some stew on to a tin plate and put it on the floor beside Rory. It smelled good, but he could only swallow a mouthful. The truth was suddenly coming to him in a rush: Cody was going to kill him. Rory had never thought of dying before; only old people died. No, that wasn't quite true: his mother wasn't old when she died. He remembered her as he had seen her last, and how he had touched her and right away wished he hadn't, because there was no warmth and life in her. And now he was going to be like that. He felt as though he would vomit.

Cody was speaking into the radio, over and over. There was no reply. He tried steadily for ten minutes. Then he stood up, swore and struck the seat with his fist.

"Easy, easy, you'll break it," said Garnett, full of stew and good humour.

"Break it? It's broken already, you fathead. We've got to get over to their camp right now! We don't dare wait until morning. We want to be on that plane at daylight."

"How far is it from here?"

"Eight or ten miles."

"That's a long walk in the dark. I've already walked five."

"If you don't want to go it's all right with me. You're nothing but trouble. I'll collect your share of the money."

"I'll go. Just give me an hour to rest. Maybe the storm will've stopped by then." Garnett lit a cigarette and tilted his chair against the wall beside the stove. He nodded at Rory. "What about him? Shall we tie him up and leave him?"

"I haven't decided yet."

"Tie him up and leave him, that's good enough. Hey, by the way, the kid says there used to be an old trapper living here."

"Do you see any old trapper living here?"

"Well, I just wondered. Suppose he comes bursting in here from his trapline all of a sudden?"

"He won't come bursting in."

"How do you know? Those guys go out for weeks at a time but sooner or later they come back with their catch, you know."

"This one won't come back."

Garnett took the cigarette from his mouth and slowly righted his chair. "What do you mean?"

"Just what I said. We won't have any more trouble with old Shredded Wheat or whatever they used to call him."

"You didn't hurt that old man, did you?" Garnett asked nervously.

"Talk, talk, talk, you never know when to stop talking," Cody said furiously. "All right, I'll tell you. I needed a place to hide out near the rig, right? I told the old guy I wanted to stay here. I knew he hated Millard's guts. He said it was fine with him, he'd already messed up some of WestCan's trucks and he'd do anything else to make life miserable for Millard."

Rory perked up a little. So that accounted for the broken-down trucks. But where was Cornflakes now?

"Then he started getting ornery," Cody went on. "He said I was getting in his way. I told him I was staying. So he took off across the clearing hollering that he was going to tell Millard everything. So I had to shoot him."

"You *what*?"

"I tried to scare him with a shot over his head but he didn't scare. Then I aimed for the leg, just to bring him down. Well, I shot higher than I figured."

"You *murdered* him!"

"Take it easy. He didn't have a friend in the world. He never went to town for months at a time. He won't be missed until spring. By that time, I figure the wolves will have cleaned up the evidence."

"I don't want any part of this," Garnett said, getting up. "I sure didn't figure on this."

"Sit down and shut up!" Cody rose menacingly. "You haven't got a choice, mister. You're in this whole thing with me."

"I got in this to bail myself out of gambling debts. I sure don't mean to get tagged for murder!"

"Look, mister, when I took on this job I didn't figure on killing anybody either! It was an accident. But it's done now and I'm going to claim my money tomorrow and nobody's stopping me. I have to get out of this country now and I sure won't let you foul up my plans. You can come along and keep your mouth shut or stay, whichever you like. But if you stay, I'll shut your mouth for keeps. One more dead guy makes no difference to me now."

Garnett slumped down, his head in his hands. Rory wasn't drowsy now. All the terror of that night in the clearing swept over him again. Cody was a cold-blooded murderer. He'd killed one man and he wouldn't think twice about killing a boy. Garnett wouldn't stop him.

If I can make it out the door into the dark maybe I can lose them, he thought. Even if I freeze, it's better than getting shot.

He wiggled his arms and toes. He was stiff but his feet hadn't gone to sleep or anything. He tensed his legs. His foot bumped the tin plate. Cody looked over quickly.

"Now, big-mouth, what're we going to do with you? I could take you out and lose you in the bush. You'd be frozen solid by morning." He struck a match to light a cigarette, then looked at the flame. "Or maybe you don't like the cold. Well, I could give you a little tap on the head and leave you here and burn the cabin down."

Garnett looked up and said quietly, "I don't care what they do to me, Cody, but I won't let you kill this kid."

"I told you to shut up."

"I don't care. Leave him here tied up until we get away or something. But I won't let you kill him." Garnett was on his feet, looking very big. Cody snatched a rifle from the corner, worked a cartridge into the chamber and cocked it.

"Maybe I'll just burn the two of you together," he said. The two stood, tense, eyeing one another like alley cats. Now, Rory thought, now! He sprang to his feet, stumbled

97

to the door, and was out in the blizzard. He heard Cody cry, "Stop him!" and heard the rifle go off. A bullet splintered the door jamb over his head.

He ran for the corner of the cabin, but his legs skidded out from under him in the fresh snow. He rolled over in terror. Garnett was almost over him, getting ready to lunge. Then—was he dreaming it?—a big figure loomed out of the storm. A huge fist fell like a sledge-hammer on Garnett's neck. Garnett's eyes went blank and he fell, like a bundle of laundry, over Rory.

15

Sammy on the Trail

Back at the camp that afternoon no one noticed at first that Rory was missing. When the excitement over the oil show died down, the day-shift men returned to work. Oscar Reason hurried away to study the cores. Tank Millard followed him. Kruger strolled to the office and noticed that someone had been using the two-way radio. The microphone, which looked something like a telephone receiver, was lying carelessly beside the set. He frowned and hung it up.

Lefebvre, glancing at his watch, saw that it was quarter to five and went back to the kitchen to peel potatoes. On the way he met Sammy and Annie Football.

"Where's Rory, Mr Lefebvre?"

"Oh, he's around, Sammy. Lots of excitement today."

"What happened?"

Lefebvre lowered his voice. "Can you keep a big secret?"

"Sure."

"Well, maybe, just maybe, we've found a lot of oil. But don't you tell anybody outside this camp. You promise?"

"Sure! Come on, Annie, let's find Rory."

"He might be around the rig," Lefebvre called after them. "Or in the geologist's trailer, or in the office. Hey, tell him to be sure and get over to the kitchen by five-thirty."

But Rory wasn't around the rig. Nor was he in the office trailer, nor in his own trailer. They knocked on Oscar Reason's door.

"Come in." Reason and Rory's father looked up impatiently from an oil sample of mud. "What is it, kids?"

"Please, Mr Millard, is Rory here?"

"No. He's around somewhere. Run along now. We're awfully busy."

"We've looked everywhere, Mr Millard."

99

"Oh, he must be around somewhere. Where'd he go when he left the rig, Oscar?"

"Didn't notice. I was too busy with this stuff."

Millard looked at his watch. "Just about dark. If he's wandered off again, I swear I'll tan his hide. Well, I guess I can send a preliminary report on the strength of what we have here, eh, Oscar?"

"Definitely. There's oil. Just a matter of finding out how much."

Millard walked back to the office trailer. "I have to call our office. Then we'll have a look for Rory if he hasn't shown up." Dutch Kruger looked up when they entered.

"I'm going to phone our people, Dutch. I'll use the scrambler on the phone, so nobody else can pick up the news. This is one report I'll enjoy!"

"Uh-huh. Say, were you on the radio a while ago?"

"No. Haven't used it since the last time the Otter flew in."

"Oh? Funny. When I came back it looked as though somebody had been using it."

Millard frowned. "If you ever catch any of the crew monkeying around with it, let me know. They ought to know better than that."

Suddenly Annie Football gave a little gasp. "Mr Millard!"

"Just a minute, Annie, until I send this report."

"Oh, but this is important! Where's Mr Garnett?"

"Garnett? I've no idea. Now keep quiet while I . . ."

"But Mr Millard! He's the spy! Mr Garnett is. Rory told us. And if somebody was using the radio I bet it was him, sending a message. And I bet Rory's following him."

Tank Millard wearily turned away from the radio and looked squarely at the little girl.

"Sometimes," he said, to nobody in particular, "I wonder if this is a drill rig or the children's story hour. All right, Annie, what's on your mind?"

Quickly, she and Sammy poured out the story. "And we know it's Mr Garnett, but we didn't have any proof," Annie finished.

Tank Millard nodded. "You sure don't have any proof!

100

Footprints in the snow! This camp is full of footprints and men with big boots. Who does your grandfather think he is, Sherlock Holmes? Dutch!"

"Yes?"

"Find Garnett. Fetch him here. Let's get this nonsense settled once and for all."

"Sure."

Tank Millard waited in his chair. He said, half aloud, "Trouble, there's been nothing but trouble since I brought that boy out here. Couldn't be Jim Garnett. He's been with me three years." He looked at the children. "If this turns out to be another false alarm, I don't ever want to see you around here again. There'll be no reason to come, anyway. Your friend Rory won't be here."

He moved to the window. There was still enough daylight to see Kruger, Wirkowski and Clay running from trailer to trailer. Tank Millard frowned, pulled on his parka and went outside. Kruger trotted toward him.

"Garnett's nowhere around, Tank. Nobody's seen him since the oil show. They thought he was having coffee or in the john."

"And no sign of Rory either?"

"Afraid not."

Millard pursed his lips. "Still doesn't prove anything. But where the devil did *they* go?" Sammy and Annie had disappeared.

"Mr Millard, come quick!" Annie Football was beckoning from behind the office trailer. They ran and found Sammy kneeling in the snow, his sister peering over his shoulder.

"I was having a look around, Mr Millard, and I found these tracks."

The men followed his pointing finger.

"Just a mess of tracks," Clay said. "So what?"

"There was a man and a smaller person," Sammy said. "They were rolling around in the snow over there, see? And then over here they stopped and the tracks aren't messed up so much." Sammy rose and followed the trail. "That's funny. The boy's . . . Rory's tracks are gone." He moved into the trees. The men looked at each other, shrugged and followed. Sammy cried. "Here! Here's Rory's feet again! Garnett must have carried him here." And there were Rory's footprints, sure enough, where Garnett had set him down. Then the snow was scuffed again, where man and boy had struggled a second time. Finally, the footprints went on, man and boy together, clearly now.

"Those prints have probably been here for days," said Clay.

"No, they're new today," Sammy insisted. "See, the snow they kicked up is all fresh and powdery."

Tank Millard hesitated. "I don't know what to make of this. But we can't afford to ignore it. It's getting dark. Sammy, could you follow this trail if you had a light?"

"Sure, Mr Millard. I'm about the best tracker between here and . . ."

"Steve," Rory's father said to Wirkowski, "get a couple of flashlights, extra batteries, your rifle, some warm clothes. Quick!"

"I'll come too," Clay said.

"Thanks, but two's enough, Harvey. No use making any more noise than we can help. Dutch, you phone the office about those cores. Explain that the news might have leaked out. And, Dutch, if we're not back by daylight call the Mountie and get a search going." He looked at Clay again. "Harvey, there's one thing you can do. Take the little girl back to her folks, and explain about Sammy so they won't worry."

"Please let me go with you, Mr Millard."

"No, Annie. There might be trouble. I don't want you hurt."

They were back at camp and ready to leave again within five minutes. Sammy, Wirkowski and Rory's father retraced their steps to the point where Garnett had put Rory on his feet again. Suddenly there was a crash behind them. Wirkowski whirled round with his rifle levelled. Tank Millard swung his light into the bush. Then Annie Football stumbled into the beam, with a red-faced Clay behind her.

102

"She got away, Boss. She runs like a rabbit! Now come on back, kid."

"Please, Mr Millard." Annie was crying. "I want to go."

"Absolutely not."

"But Rory's my friend!"

Millard groaned. "I'm telling you, it's a regular kindergarten around here. Oh, all right, stay. But stay behind us. Clay, will you go tell her folks?"

"Well, sure, Tank, but I can't speak Dogrib."

"I thought you were an educated man! Listen, her father speaks English as well as I do. Let's go, Steve."

They went on, Sammy first with a flashlight, Millard next, Wirkowski behind him with the rifle, Annie in the rear. The trail showed up clearly in the beam of light and they moved on steadily until six o'clock.

"I figure we've come a little better than two miles," Rory's father said. "You kids all right?"

"Fine!" Sammy was chewing gum furiously and walking with a swagger. Annie nodded. She was holding back large tears.

"Cheer up." Tank Millard patted her shoulder. "We'll find them." But privately he was beginning to have doubts. Where was Garnett going? Slowly he was realizing that his boy, the only family he had in the world, had been snatched and carried off by a desperate man. That is, if he could believe the Indian kids. "Well, let's keep moving."

They trudged on. Six-thirty came; quarter to seven. The snow began. They looked at one another, silently, and moved faster. They knew that at this rate there would soon be no trail to follow. Seven o'clock: they had gone nearly four miles now, but the footprints were almost buried.

Seven-fifteen: Sammy stopped, wiped his nose on his sleeve and looked miserable.

"I'm sorry, Mr Millard. I just can't see a thing any more."

They huddled in a circle, backs hunched against the storm. Anne was crying again. Wirkowski swore—the first time he had spoken in two hours. Tank Millard pounded a fist into his palm. "We've got to think. What would they do? What would you do, Steve, if you were caught out in a storm like this?"

"Get under a tree, I guess."

"Maybe. Sammy, you've lived outdoors. What would you do?"

"Find shelter and build a fire. No good to curl up in the snow: you'd freeze. If there weren't any old cabins around I'd make a lean-to out of branches and . . ."

"The cabin!" cried Annie. "Cornflakes's cabin!"

"What?"

"Cornflakes's cabin. It's around here somewhere."

"Would Garnett or Rory know that?"

"Rory might. We sneaked up on it once."

"Well, it's worth a try. Can you find it, Sammy?"

Sammy frowned. "We've wandered around so much and it's so dark . . ." He stood silently, studying the private map of the bush country that he carried in his head. "Yeah. Yeah, I think I know. We just keep on in the same direction we've been going."

He darted off into the storm, weaving in and out among the trees, not bothering to look at the ground any more but playing his light on the trees around him. Once he paused, held the beam on a curious twisted spruce and gave a little grunt of satisfaction. "Not far now."

Five minutes later, at nearly eight o'clock, he stopped at the edge of a clearing. "There." He pointed. The cabin light showed dimly through a curtain of snow.

"Well, I'll be a monkey's uncle! Sammy, you're a wizard." Tank Millard squeezed his arm. "Now, Steve, you circle up on one side and I'll take the other. We'll take a peek first and see what's in there. If that old trapper's still mad at us we might have to be careful. Sammy, Annie, don't move until I tell you to."

The men slipped away in opposite directions. In a moment Sammy and Annie saw their dark shadows at either corner of the cabin. Suddenly a muffled shot rang from inside. Before they could move in, the door burst open and Rory tumbled out. Annie opened her mouth to call him but Sammy hissed, "Quiet!" For then Garnett plunged out too.

They saw Wirkowski step out and drop Garnett with one blow to the back of the neck, as casually as though he were swatting a fly. Then Tank Millard charged the cabin door—and ran head-on into Vic Cody, rifle in hand.

16

The Last Fight

For a split second Cody was too astonished to move. It was long enough for Rory's father to shove the rifle barrel aside. Then Cody squeezed the trigger but the bullet whined harmlessly into the trees. With a wrench that almost twisted Cody's fingers off, Tank Millard tore the rifle away. The man yelped with pain. Millard drove a fist into his midriff with an underhand swing that started behind his back. Cody's grunt echoed across the clearing. He stumbled back through the cabin doorway with Tank Millard pressing in after him.

Outside, Wirkowski had his part of the situation well in hand. Garnett was sitting up, his eyes glazed, with no more interest in the fight. Rory scrambled shakily to his feet and leaned against the cabin wall. Sammy and Annie capered out of the snow like little white ghosts and ran to his side. Cautiously they peered in the cabin door.

Cody was back on his feet now. Rory's father moved in and the scout kicked out desperately. Tank Millard doubled up, clutching his stomach. Cody kicked again, a glancing blow to the face. Rory's father fell backward, bleeding at the mouth, but he was up again in an instant. They circled the room, crouching. It was their fight and no one else's. Outside, Wirkowski was trying to keep watch on his prisoner while peering in to see if his boss needed help.

Cody made the first move, a lunging blow at the head. Tank Millard ducked and swung his whole body behind a smash to the ribs. The scout dropped his hands. Rory had never seen his father so angry. Millard swung again, a wicked jab that closed Cody's left eye, then another piledriver to the chest. Cody fell heavily against the stove. It toppled with a crash of pipes and a shower of red embers. Cody screamed as one of them seared through his shirt.

Instantly the room was full of smoke. The stove had

spilled over a stack of yellowing magazines and now flames were running up the back wall. The two men tumbled out of the cabin, Cody first, Millard on his heels; Cody kept on going. He crossed the clearing on the dead run before Wirkowski could raise his rifle.

"Get him!" Tank Millard yelled, and Wirkowski plunged off into the night. But he was back a moment later.

"Can't see a thing," he bellowed. "Gimme a flashlight!"

"Wait a minute, let's get organized." Millard turned to Rory. "Are you all right?"

"Yes. I . . . I guess you're mad."

"No. No, just glad you're all right. How much does Cody know?"

"Everything. Garnett's been sending information all along. He tried to radio him this afternoon, but he couldn't get him. That's why he came over here."

"Cody tell anybody else?"

"He tried, by radio, a while ago. He couldn't get anybody."

"Who's he dealing with?"

"Some oil company that has men eight or ten miles from here."

"That'll be where Cody's headed now," Rory's father said grimly. "I've got to stop him." He looked at Garnett, shivering in his shirt-sleeves. "One thing about it, Cody forgot to take his parka. He'll be getting pretty chilly. Now, where's your coat? Near the door?"

Garnett nodded. The cabin was blazing now, but Tank Millard stepped to the door, shielded his face with one arm and fumbled inside for the coat pegs. In a minute he was out, coughing, but triumphantly holding up Cody's and Garnett's parkas. Garnett gratefully huddled into his.

"Steve," said Tank Millard. "You stay here with him and the kids. I'm going after Cody." He looked hesitantly at Sammy. "On second thought . . . Sammy, are you game for a few more miles? I could sure use you for a tracker."

"Sure," Sammy said.

"Me, too," said Rory. "I want to see Cody caught."

"Aren't you tired?"

"Not that tired."

Rory's father looked at him proudly. "You've tough-

108

ened up a lot. Sure you can come. This is your show, more than anybody's. Let's go."

Then they were out in the bush again, moving with a whispering of feet through the soft snow. Tank Millard had a rifle; Sammy and Rory, the flashlights. The blizzard was almost over, and Sammy soon picked up Cody's half-filled tracks. At first, the man had lunged along in long, frightened strides, glancing off trees and bushes. Then, as he realized he was not being followed and as his eyes grew accustomed to the night, he had settled down, changed course, apparently heading for his employers' camp, and moved along steadily. But within a mile the footprints grew more distinct. He was not far ahead and was evidently feeling the cold. The trail stopped from time to time, always in the shelter of a bush.

"He's getting pretty miserable," Tank Millard grunted. "Ten below is no weather for shirt-sleeves. I figure he'll be pretty tame when we catch him."

They pushed on.

"Real close," said Sammy in a low voice. "I can tell by the trail. Real close!"

"Keep flashing your light ahead," Rory's father warned. "And stay close to me. He hasn't got a gun but he could still be pretty tough."

They passed through a heavy stand of trees. Suddenly Sammy hissed, "No more trail!" He swung his light along the snow. But there was no sign of Cody.

Tank Millard started to say, "Watch it, he must be hid . . ." when Rory, arcing his flashlight beam overhead, suddenly shouted, "Dad, duck!"

Tank Millard's reflexes were good, and this saved his life. He ducked instantly, down and to one side just as Cody dropped heavily from a branch. Even so, he landed partly on the rig boss's back, driving him to his knees. But the vicious sweep of the knife—they'd forgotten that Cody would have a knife—missed Tank Millard's throat and merely tore through the shoulder and sleeve of his thick parka.

Then Tank Millard yanked the knife hand with a jerk that brought Cody head-first over his shoulder. Cody gasped, dropped the knife, but wriggled free and made one last desperate try, a dive for Tank Millard's fallen rifle. He clutched it awkwardly in his numbed fingers, just as Tank swung an uppercut that caught the oil scout full in the face. Cody fell like a tree, blood running from his nose.

Rory's father gathered up the rifle and examined his shoulder. The knife had left a long scratch down his arm, nothing more.

He rubbed a fistful of snow vigorously in Cody's face and brought him around. Then they trudged wearily back to the cabin, which by now was merely a smouldering shell. Wirkowski had started a small fire in the clearing; the others were waiting round it.

Tank Millard tossed Cody his parka, and squatted beside the fire. "We'll rest a little, then go back. There's no use trying to sleep here. Too miserable." He looked at Garnett for the first time since they had rescued Rory. "So you were selling us out, Jim? How come?"

Garnett didn't look big and handsome any more, just frightened and miserable and sick. "I lost a few thousand bucks to some guys in the city over the Christmas holidays. They were pressing me for it, Tank, I mean really pressing. They threatened me. Cody knew about it and he offered me a deal. I just had to have that money, Tank."

Rory's father turned away in disgust. Rory said, "There's something else. The other one killed Cornflakes." He repeated Cody's story. "He was going to kill me too. He was talking about leaving me in the woods to freeze." Rory couldn't keep a quiver out of his voice. "Or—burning down the cabin with me in it."

The tears welled up in Annie's eyes again. "Oh, Rory, that's awful!"

"The kid's lying," said Cody. His face was bloody and badly swollen but he was his old mean scowling self again.

"No, he's not," Garnett said. "It's the truth. But I didn't go along with any of that, Tank. I'm no killer."

"That's right, Dad. He didn't want Cody to hurt me."

"You didn't do much to prevent it, though, Jim. You brought Rory here."

"But there was no choice . . ."

"You mean it was the easiest way out. You always look

110

for the easy way, don't you, Jim? I'm sorry for you. I really am."

Then Garnett did a strange thing for a grown man: he broke down and sobbed. It was embarrassing and everybody looked away, except Cody.

"Well, would you lookit that," he sneered. "How'd I ever get mixed up with a marshmallow like this one? Even the kid didn't cry."

"No," Rory's father said. "I don't expect he did." He looked at Rory with a little smile, the first time he'd done that for weeks. "He's more of a man than Garnett, and smarter than a lot of grownups."

He looked back at Cody. "As for you, tough guy, talk it up while you can. Your talking days are about over." The fire was burning low. "Well, do you think we can make it back to the rig, people? Can we find the way?"

"Sure we can," Rory said. "Sammy Football's the best darn tracker between here and Aklavik."

Sammy grinned. Annie chuckled. Tank Millard, to Rory's amazement, laughed out loud. Even Wirkowski managed a grin. Sammy fished in his pocket, found a slightly used wad of Wrigley's Doublemint, popped it into his mouth and led the way back to Rory's wildcat.

17

Goodbye to the Wildcat

"Last time you do this, Rory!" Lefebvre looked up from the stove. The kitchen smelled richly of peas and baked potatoes and roast beef. "It is pretty sad when a fellow has to help make his own farewell dinner. But there you are—you see how bad I need you around here? You better not go back to Edmonton."

"I wish I didn't have to, René. But Dad has to go down to the trial. And I have to go in to write exams. I got way behind with my work the last little while too, so if I don't finish up at a real school, I might flunk my whole year."

"Well, it sure hasn't been much good for studying around here the last couple of weeks, I'll say that."

Ten days had gone by. Cody and Garnett were in jail in Edmonton. The new well was even better than anyone had dared to hope. With the secret kept, WestCan had fared well at the land sale. Three more WestCan rigs were on the way in, hurrying to beat the spring thaw. Tomorrow Rory's wildcat would come down and move to another site.

And today—well, today was the end of it all, a sad and exciting day. There would be guests for dinner. The company's Twin Otter was flying in any minute now. It was bringing the president of WestCan, all the way from Calgary to see the new well, that's how important it was. After dinner he would fly back to Edmonton with Rory and his father.

"Well, I'll send you off with a good dinner," Lefebvre said. "Roast beef, baked potatoes, peas, mushrooms, squash . . ."

"I don't like squash."

"You'd better like this. I cook a good squash. . . . And ice cream and strawberries."

"I'm glad Sammy and Annie can come," said Rory. "I'm sure going to miss them. And you too, René."

"Well, hey Rory, you will just have to come back on summer holidays. Hey, I hear that Otter."

The aircraft circled the camp, then settled gently out of sight beyond the trees.

Then the jeep bounced into camp with Kruger at the wheel and the pilot, his engineer, and another man inside. The man didn't look much like a president was supposed to. He wore a parka, like anybody else, and he was tall and gangling with big hands and a big nose. He unfolded himself from the jeep and met Rory's father who was hurrying over from the silent rig.

"Well, Tank. I guess you know everybody is damn excited about this."

"I feel good about it myself, Dan, especially since we had more than the usual amount of trouble before it came in."

"Yes, I've heard all about the business with the scout." Their voices faded as they strolled to the well-head together. Rory turned back to meet Sammy and Annie, who were coming down the road. The Footballs were shy and subdued. They went into the kitchen and took off their parkas. Annie had substituted a pink dress for her usual blue jeans and she wore a pink ribbon in her glossy hair.

"Hey! You look like a girl!" Lefebvre cried. Annie blushed.

"And Sammy looks lovely, too," said Lefebvre. "Sammy, you look pretty!"

"Aw, quit it, Mr Lefebvre!" Sammy was squirming in a new blue plaid shirt and a clean pair of blue jeans. His hair, watered and brushed, stood up in layers like a thatched roof.

Rory's father and the man named Dan sat down with the crew. There was an awkward silence at first, but then the stranger told a story about a time when he was a driller at Leduc. It turned out that Dutch Kruger had been a roughneck there a year or two later, and pretty soon the whole table was talking easily about oil drilling and the price of new cars.

On the way out, the president stopped beside Sammy. "I heard how you helped Mr Millard. We certainly appreciate that."

Sammy grinned and shuffled his feet.

"Do you go to school?"

"Yessir. Well, sometimes."

"What are you going to do when you grow up?"

"I guess I'll be a mechanic. Or a hockey player. Or maybe work on one of those drill rigs."

"I see. And what about your sister? Annie, is it? What would you like to do, Annie?"

"I *think* I want to be a teacher."

"Mmm. Well, maybe we can do something to help." He patted Annie's head and said, "I'll see you on the plane, Rory."

Then it was time to say goodbye, to Lefebvre, to Clay, to big gruff Wirkowski, to all the men Rory had grown to know and like in that long time—was it only three months he'd been there? Dutch Kruger and the Footballs drove them to the waiting plane.

There, Rory said awkwardly, "Well, so long. I'll try to get back in the summer." Annie's eyes were brimming with tears. Sammy wiped his nose on his mitten and cleared his throat noisily. "I could teach you how to fish, y'know. I'm real good at it."

Then the Otter bounced down the home-made runway and up, up over the treetops. It swung round in a wide arc and Rory could see the jeep and the little specks beside it that were his two best friends in all the world. The Otter turned south and Rory's wildcat was only a dot in the bush.

He settled back in a seat across from his father and the other man. Well, now what? he wondered. His father had been a lot friendlier in the last few days. But when the trial was over he'd go back to the bush as always. Rory would be alone again, without even Lefebvre and Sammy and Annie. He'd have to stay in school; studying in a drill camp just didn't work. He had never in his life felt so alone, not even that first day in the Fort Mackenzie restaurant.

His father and the man were talking. Out of habit, Rory scrunched himself down and closed his eyes. Sure enough, they were soon talking as though he weren't there.

"What about the little Indian kids, Tank?"

115

"They're a smart pair."

"I'd like to see them get more schooling. Any chance?"

"It's not easy. Some of the parents don't put as much importance on schooling as we do. Sometimes they take a little trip into the bush and take the kids along. Sure, you could put the kids in a town and make sure they got to school, but it'd have to be close to the parents. Because they're real family people."

"Better than we are, maybe?"

Tank Millard looked sharply at the other man. "Well . . . I must say they spend more time with their children than I ever have."

"See what you can do to help. If it costs the company a little money, that's all right."

"I'll see."

"What about you? Don't you get tired of wandering? You don't have to, you know."

"I'd be no good pushing a pencil across a desk in Calgary, Dan."

"What about your son? It's not fair to him, you being away so much."

"I know. It has me worried."

"How would you like to run WestCan's new regional office in Fort Mackenzie? You could put Rory in school there—they're opening a new school next fall, I hear— and you could get out into the bush often enough to keep yourself happy."

Rory's heart leaped. He'd be closer to Annie and Sammy. Maybe he could even talk his father into giving Matthew Football a job in town—then Annie and Sammy could go to the same school! And his father would be home most of the time. If only he would say yes to the company president!

Tank Millard was saying in surprised tones, "Why, I didn't even know you were starting a new office!"

"It's not announced yet but, yes. This oil play is going to open up this part of the country."

"And you want me to run it? That sounds great. That's very good of you, Dan."

"I'm not doing it to be nice. You're the best man for

116

the job. Nobody could boss a big drilling program as well as you."

"All right, I accept. I *would* like to spend more time with the boy. You know, we're just starting to get acquainted for the first time in our lives. I used to think he was soft. But he's not. If anything, he's too stubborn."

The company president laughed, a low rumbling sort of laugh. "It sounds to me as though he's exactly like his father."

Rory looked over, through squinted eyes. His father looked startled and then a little pleased. He said, "You know, I guess you're right!" And he threw back his head and laughed. It was the second time in ten days he'd laughed like that.

Hey, thought Rory, things are really looking up.

About the Author

Robert Collins was born on a farm near Shamrock, Sask. He served three years in the R.C.A.F. during World War II and graduated in journalism from the University of Western Ontario in 1950. Since then, his jobs have included: western editor of *Maclean's* Magazine (five years), editor of *Imperial Oil Review* (seven years), editor of *Toronto Life* Magazine and, for the last five years, roving editor of *Reader's Digest* (Canada). Robert Collins has won seven national awards for magazine writing and has published eight books.